THE TEXAS RANGER'S DAUGHTER

Jenna Kernan

First published in Great Britain 2013
by Mills & Boon, an imprint of Harlequin (UK) Limited.
Harlequin (UK) Limited, Eton House, 18-24 Paradise Road,
Richmond, Surrey TW9 1SR

ISBN: 978 0 263 89810 1

Harlequin (UK) policy is to use papers that are natural, renewable and recyclable products and made from wood grown in sustainable forests. The logging and manufacturing process conform to the legal environmental regulations of the country of origin.

Printed and bound in Spain
by Blackprint CPI, Barcelona

Every bit as adventurous as her heroines, **Jenna Kernan** is an avid gold-prospector, searching America's gold-bearing rivers for elusive nuggets. She and her husband have written several books on gem and mineral hunting. Her debut novel, WINTER WOMAN, was a RITA® Award finalist for Best First Book.

Jenna lives with her husband and two bad little parrots in New York. Visit her on the web at www.jennakernan.com, for news, contests and excerpts.

Previous novels by Jenna Kernan:

WINTER WOMAN
TURNER'S WOMAN
HIS BROTHER'S BRIDE
  (part of *Wed Under Western Skies*)
THE TRAPPER
FALLEN ANGEL
  (part of *A Western Winter Wonderland*)
HIGH PLAINS BRIDE
OUTLAW BRIDE
SIERRA BRIDE
HIS DAKOTA CAPTIVE
THE SHERIFF'S HOUSEKEEPER BRIDE
  (part of *Western Winter Wedding Bells*)
GOLD RUSH GROOM

To Jim—now and always.

Chapter One

Northwest of San Antonio, Texas, 1879

The men watched her with hungry eyes. Laurie Bender sat perfectly still outside the circle of firelight, hands bound before her, praying to disappear, knowing from the long, lustful stares that not one of the outlaws had forgotten about her.

She had endured a night and day of hell since her abduction from the train station in San Antonio. She'd been bound, tied and bounced over rough country in the back of a buckboard until she was black-and-blue. But that would be nothing compared to what awaited her next.

She cast a quick glance around the circle

to find the biggest ruffian staring at her. The instant their eyes met, he rubbed his groin in the most lewd gesture she had ever seen. She dropped her gaze but could not contain her gasp of shock. The blood drained from her face so fast that her cheeks tingled and her ears began to ring. His laughter raised the hairs on her neck; it was a cruel sound filled with malice and menace. From then on, Laurie kept her eyes on the fire.

If only her father would come before it was too late. Had her letter reached him? Did he even know to expect her?

"Rider!"

The shout came from the ridge above the outlaws' filthy little camp, squatting against the cliff of a box canyon around the remains of a broken-down adobe ranch house. The structure now lacked a roof and had been abandoned, Laurie supposed, for lack of one single thing a ranch needed.

All nine men set aside their bottles and rose to their feet, drawing their guns in unison. Three melted into the darkness while the others fanned out. Two mounted up and rode past the second sentry, who was perched high on the cliff above them.

The big one in the gray hat took the opportunity to come straight at her. He grabbed her hair as one might grasp a troublesome weed and yanked, forcing her head back.

He nuzzled against her neck above the top of the knife-pleated ruffle that topped her blouse and then brought his lips to her ear.

"I'm taking you now," he growled.

A pistol cocked close to Laurie's head and the man let go so fast she stumbled.

"I like ya, Larson. I do. But I can't abide a man not following orders." It was the voice of their leader, George Hammer. Laurie recognized it, would never forget it as long as she lived. Everyone in Texas had heard of George Hammer and his gang because he killed all witnesses of each robbery he committed down to the last woman and child. His soul must be as black as ink. Laurie knew he would be punished in the afterlife, but that belief was cold comfort now.

Her father was one of the men after Hammer. Laurie closed her eyes, imagining her father's division of Texas Rangers storming the camp.

The painful grip on her hair eased away and her scalp tingled in relief as Larson stepped back.

"Been a long time since we had a woman, boss," Larson whined.

"Now you apologize to our little guest." The outlaw stood with Larson, moving in a slow-motion pantomime that made Laurie's heart pound.

Hammer held the cocked pistol barrel pressed to his underling's forehead. Larson didn't seem to be breathing, but he sure was sweating. Laurie wondered how *he* liked being so afraid he couldn't draw breath? Suddenly he didn't look so tough.

"'Pologize!" demanded Hammer.

Larson's eyes shifted to her and she read the glittering hatred there. She prayed he would not have opportunity to seek revenge against her for this perceived grievance. She lifted her chin in defiance, feigning a bravery she did not feel, trying still to be her father's daughter.

"Yes, ma'am. I sure do. I sure am sorry."

"Now git," said Hammer, prodding him with the cold steel. Larson toppled like a falling tree, landed on his backside in the dust and then scuttled away like a scorpion. Laurie noted the pink ring mark on the outlaw's forehead, the imprint of George Hammer's pistol.

George Hammer grabbed Laurie's bound hands and squatted, drawing them both back to a seat on the log, as if they were good friends, except he kept a fist on the ropes, squeezing so the bonds rubbed her chafed skin. All the while he kept that pleasant smile fixed upon his lips. Laurie shivered.

"Time for that later, I reckon," he said, watching Larson disappear from the circle of light cast by the fire. Then he returned his gaze to her.

He looked her over with a critical eye and nodded. Laurie realized his smile never reached his eyes. Oh, no. His eyes were flat and lifeless as smoked glass.

"You don't look much like him. He don't have your dark hair or eyes. Your ma as pretty as you?"

She looked away in answer and learned her mistake when he grasped her chin and wrenched her forward to look at him.

"You know what your pa done to my kin?"

Laurie shook her head, anxiety sitting heavy in her belly, but she kept her posture straight, due for the most part to the long-boned corset that reached her hips, supporting her now that her spine proved unable to do so. She'd lost her straw hat and her upswept hair now tumbled in a dark tangle over one shoulder. Hammer settled beside her and stared off into the camp instead of at her. "Because of him, I had to bring my little brother home to our mama with his tongue all swollen and purple. Wasn't a proper hanging, just strung him up on his horse, so it didn't break his neck." The outlaw stroked Laurie's throat, washing her insides with cold terror. His grip tightened. "He strangled real slow. That's a hard death. Your pa did that."

Her voice croaked like a frog's. "I'm sorry for your loss."

He released her hands and gave them a gentle pat. He turned to face her, letting her see his bloodshot eyes narrowing on her with hatred. "You will be. I'll see to that. Time your pa gets here, there won't be much left." He snorted. "I mean to have justice. Promised my ma I'd make him pay. My little brother for his little girl. But we won't kill ya." He leaned in, so that her nose nearly touched his big greasy one. "But you'll wish we would." He glanced toward his men, all waiting for the rider. "First I'll let 'em get drunk, real drunk. Drunk men ain't gentle." He gave her knee a little squeeze. "'Spect they'll pass you around with the bottle. Gonna be a long night. So you best rest up."

She could hear hoofbeats now. Someone shouted.

"It's Boon. He's alone."

The men holstered their guns, except Hammer.

"You take his pistols?" asked their leader.

"Yeah," called one of the riders, holding up a holster with its weapon still sheathed within.

Three riders trotted into the circle of men. It wasn't her father or one of his Rangers. Her disappointment weighed down upon her. If she'd had a way to take her own life she surely would have. But George Hammer had taken even that, since he left her nothing with which to save herself from ruination.

Laurie's attention went to the new arrival. He rode a shod bay quarter horse with a white blaze down its nose and entered the camp at a slow walk as if he owned the place. The rider's lean body was sheathed in a tan canvas duster. A gray hat with a wide flat brim shaded his face. Beneath he wore a navy blue work shirt, fawn-colored kerchief, a scarred leather vest and dark striped trousers tucked into narrow black boots with pointed toes that fit neatly into the stirrups. He swung gracefully from the saddle, holding the reins as he lifted his gaze and scanned the group of men. Each stood at alert, hands poised to reach for their guns. Was this unarmed man so dangerous?

Laurie glanced to the rider's narrow hips, noticing he wore no holster but had maintained possession of a knife, judging from the antler handle protruding from the top of his right boot.

Boon stepped closer, approaching Hammer. He had a square jaw covered with dark whiskers that didn't obscure the cleft. He lifted his chin and now she could see his face. Her breath caught as she realized he was young and handsome. His size, confident manner and liquid grace had fooled her into assuming he was older, but he seemed to be her own age, perhaps only eighteen or nineteen. The firelight cast his bronze skin orange, but she could see his eyes were pale, like seawater.

"Thought you was dead, Boon." George Hammer stepped forward, grabbed Boon's collar and tugged, exposing his neck. "Don't see no rope burns." He pushed him away.

Boon caught himself easily and his spurs jangled. Laurie noticed one hand ball to a fist before he relaxed, stretching out his long fingers.

"Why ain't you dead?"

Boon met the outlaw's gaze with a steady one of his own.

"Don't know. My horse fell on me. Don't recall what came next. When I woke up you fellers were gone and the Rangers, too."

Hammer narrowed his eyes, his long nose nearly touching Boon's. "They caught Wilson. How'd you get away?"

Boon gave an easy shrug. "Caught my horse and rode the other way."

So he was an outlaw, just like the rest of them. Laurie's hopes flagged. Why had she let his beautiful face make her think he could not be a criminal? She had enough experience to know that looks were no indication of whether a man or woman was good or bad.

Cal stepped into the light. This was Hammer's second in command, a short, lean man. His trimmed goatee, air of authority and Southern accent all made Laurie wonder if he had been an officer for the Confederacy from one of the original secessionist states, Virginia or Georgia perhaps.

He approached Boon, circling him as if Boon was a recruit called out for inspection.

"They *shot* your horse, Boon," said Cal.

"But they didn't kill him. I did that, riding toward San Antonio. Bled to death not four miles from the last stage station. Told the station master I got bushwhacked by Comanche."

"Damn fine horse, that," said Hammer, straightening up, a note of remorse in his voice. "Fast as prairie lightning."

"He was that."

Hammer's mouth twitched. Laurie found herself holding her breath, though why she should care whether Hammer believed this man's story, she did not know.

"You been gone awhile."

Boon nodded. "Had to steal a horse and I ran into some trouble over the saddle."

Hammer whirled, closing the distance between them. "Trouble?"

Laurie inched farther from the circle, praying for some opportunity to run. They had secured her wrists in front of her, but left her legs free. If she could get up on that horse she might get away in the dark. She was a good rider, or had been, in what now seemed another lifetime.

Hammer grabbed the front of Boon's shirt in his fist. Boon didn't cower the way Larson had, nor did he lift a hand to defend himself.

"You bring anyone this way and I'll skin you alive."

"I left that deputy in Abilene. Lay low for

a few days. Been looking for you ever since. Tried the holdup we used north of San Antonio but found no sign. I thought that was where you was all heading."

Hammer released him and scratched the stubble on his chin as he eyed Boon. "Changed our mind after you went missing. Those damned Rangers hung Wilson."

Boon flicked his gaze at her. She stopped moving, frozen like a rabbit as her heart pounded in her throat. He held her gaze an instant longer then turned his attention back to their leader.

"Bender and his men."

Laurie's ears perked up at the mention of her father's name.

"Hung Wilson from a mesquite tree on the Brazos. Now I'm looking to hurt him bad. Got the opportunity when Freet here robbed a mail stage. Lucky Cal reads so good. Found us a letter from this little missy here." Hammer stroked her head and Laurie pulled away. Hammer laughed.

"Told us your train and when to meet you. Didn't you, Laurie?"

So that's how they found her. Laurie felt so stupid she could die. Probably would die. Why hadn't she noticed her escort was no Ranger?

She should have noticed. Her father certainly would have.

"She's my revenge. Going to be sweet, too." He raised his voice to a yell. "Ain't she, boys?"

The men hollered and whistled while Laurie shivered as if she stood naked before them.

Hammer glanced to Laurie and she went hot and cold until her body seemed to vibrate like struck iron. Hammer patted Boon on the shoulder and led him a few steps away. "Spent some time at a new place outside of Wichita Falls rustling cattle, but too much law over that way so we came west again." Hammer released his hold on Boon's shoulder, that terrible, pleasant smile still fixed on his face. "You get your horse settled and come back. We'll talk about you joining up again. You bring anything?"

Boon nodded, sticking his thumbs beneath his belt. "When do I get my gun back?"

George held Boon's gaze. Boon didn't look away as the others always did. Hammer didn't like that kind of challenge, so the outlaw drew his gun and aimed his weapon at the young man's middle.

Boon held his easy stance, giving no indication he was frightened. George laughed.

"I think I'll keep your pistol for a while, Boon. You understand."

Boon nodded. The man was either the coolest customer Laurie had ever seen or just plain crazy.

The young outlaw turned back to his escorts and motioned with his fingers. The guard who'd accompanied him into the camp made a face, glanced at their leader and then handed over a Winchester repeater. Laurie recognized it, for it was similar to the model her father had given her for her tenth birthday, back when they were best friends instead of strangers.

Boon offered the repeater, butt first, to Hammer.

"Took it off a cowpoke who tried to stop me taking one of their beeves."

Hammer nodded, an absent smile returning to his face. He accepted the offering, spun and aimed at the men standing by the fire, shooting one round after another. The dust at their feet flew up as the men dove behind the ring of logs.

"Seems to fire a little low," said Hammer conversationally to Boon.

"Every weapon takes getting used to," he answered.

Hammer nodded, using the lever to expel

the final empty round, and then relaxed his arm so that the weapon now hung at his side.

The outlaws dusted off their trousers and chaps as Hammer turned toward the dilapidated house. Laurie saw her opportunity, bolted to her feet and ran toward the horse Boon had vacated. She leaped and Boon caught her in midair, spinning her around as he captured her in his strong arms. He brought her back to the ground, keeping hold of her, pressing her back against his chest so she faced the others.

He held her as she struggled, his body hard and his grip unbreakable.

George Hammer stalked back to Laurie, opened his hand and slapped her across the face. The sting of the slap made her eyes water, but the damage could have been much worse had her captor not pulled her away from the direction of the blow the instant the outlaw struck.

Laurie blinked in shock, waiting for the second blow, but George Hammer seemed oblivious to what had just happened.

He narrowed his eyes on Boon and raised his voice. "Least one of my men ain't too drunk or too stupid to make himself useful."

He whirled and kicked at the closest man, but he dodged, scrambling backward over the log.

"She gets away and I kill someone." He stalked toward the house.

Laurie turned her head to look back at her captor. His face was cold and grim, his jaw muscles bulged.

"Thank you," she whispered.

"Shut up," he growled then grabbed her elbow and dragged her back to the logs, pressing her into place none too gently. "Don't move."

He left her to return to his horse and released the girth before swinging the saddle free and setting it on the rail beside the others. Then he rubbed the gelding down with a hank of dried grass, before setting him loose in the paddock.

One of the men sat too close to Laurie. She inched away. His breath stank of rotting teeth as he lifted a lock of her hair and rubbed it between his dirty fingers. She tried to pull back, but he jerked the hank of hair. When she cried out he laughed.

Laurie glanced to Boon and noted his eyes shift, but he made no move to help her. So she faced the man herself.

"Are you trying to get shot? Hammer said no one is to touch me."

He stopped laughing, narrowing his eyes on her. Laurie held her breath. Their leader had not exactly told his men not to touch her. She waited to see what he'd do.

He took another swallow of whiskey and then rose to his feet, making a show of adjusting himself before joining the others. The men now sat on one side of the fire and she on the other, predators facing their captured prey.

She had never felt more alone in her life. The fear choked her and she grew dizzy from the worry. She knew what would come next and the dread made her nauseous.

She sat still and watchful as the men passed the whiskey and got louder and meaner by the minute.

The outlaws ate, scraping their beans and bacon off tin plates with day-old biscuits. But no one fed her. Laurie's stomach growled as she watched them, hoping for a chance to run again into the night.

At last George Hammer reemerged from the hovel of a house with Cal.

"So, who's first, boys?"

Laurie swallowed back the bile rising in

her stomach. The time had come. She glanced frantically about for somewhere to run.

But the men weren't looking at her, they were eyeing each other, sizing up the competition.

She rose, but Cal shoved her to the ground. "You're not going anywhere."

Laurie sank in the dust, leaning back against the log, and watched the men. Some hung back, remaining in their places. Others stood casually, as if just preparing to take a stroll.

Boon stepped into the firelight, the first to stake a claim.

"Me," he said, lowering his chin in a challenge.

The others glanced from one to the next, but no one stepped forward. Laurie began to tremble, her eyes darting from one to another, searching desperately for escape and finding none.

Larson finally moved from the group. He was older, bigger and outweighed the younger man by fifty pounds. But he was a coward inside; Laurie knew it from the exchange she'd seen with Hammer. Cowards didn't fight unless they were certain they could win. Cowards made the best bullies and suddenly she could not draw breath. What if it were Larson? She'd rather die, but Hammer had not given her that option.

He meant to have his pound of flesh.

She knew Larson was fully capable of breaking a man's jaw with one punch and she wondered why Boon looked so lackadaisical. The others moved to form a ring, grinning and shouting, perhaps hoping that the fight would take out one or both of them, leaving an open field. Cal rose to gain a better vantage point, leaving her unattended, just outside the ring of cheering men.

Larson lifted his fists. "Still time to back down."

Boon shook his head.

Laurie's stomach tightened. Help was not coming. She needed to do for herself or die in the attempt. She tried to think what a Ranger would do and wondered if she might sneak away in the melee. But at that moment, George Hammer sat beside her, drawing his gun and then crossing his arms so the pistol pointed casually at her.

"You just sit back down now and watch the show. You'll *be* the show soon enough. I hope it's Larson. He's big and mean as a bull. Like him to be your first. But you'll take them all, some more than once. By the time the sun's up, you'll be begging me for this bullet." He lifted the barrel of his gun. "My, your daddy will be grieved."

His smile was a bitter combination of warm satisfaction and icy vengeance. Laurie struggled not to vomit as terror gripped her belly.

The men circled each other. She could not draw her eyes from them, one slender, muscular and quick, one slow, beefy and enormous. Who would be the first to rape her?

Chapter Two

Laurie tried to draw up her knees to her chest, but her corset and bustle prevented her, so she inclined to the side, legs tucked under her skirt with one elbow resting on the log behind her as she watched. Time seemed to slow as Larson swung a bone-crushing fist at Boon's head and missed. Boon, smaller and faster, ducked, then landed a blow to Larson's ribs before spinning away as the older man bellowed. Another swing and another miss. This time Boon used his elbow to strike the back of Larson's head.

Both men were dirty fighters, but Boon was faster and stayed out of the man's reach. If Larson got his hands on him, Laurie felt certain Boon would be finished. The bigger man made a grab for his opponent and Boon used the heel of his hand against his rival's nose. The crunch made Laurie gag. His broken nose gushed blood down his indigo denim shirt and greasy brown vest. A moment later, Larson's left eye swelled shut and the big man began to stagger. He drew his gun. The men ceased cheering and dived for cover at the exact moment Boon lunged at Larson's legs, using his body like a rolling barrel to take the man down.

Laurie didn't know when it happened but she found herself rooting for Boon, clearly the underdog. What was the matter with her? She should hope they all killed each other and left her in peace.

Boon sprang to his feet and used his boot heel to crush Larson's shooting hand, still clutching the pistol. The downed man howled like a feral animal as his fingers crunched. Boon retrieved the gun from the ground.

He aimed it at Larson. The man stopped screaming and cradled his mangled hand to his chest. Boon cocked the trigger.

The clearing now fell so silent, Laurie could hear the burning logs crackle and pop in the fire.

George Hammer rose and stepped forward. The men parted as he approached. He glanced coldly at Larson, lying like a defeated gladiator in the ring. Laurie recalled this was his pick and shivered. Hammer turned his head and narrowed his eyes on Boon. The younger outlaw was so still, he seemed carved of marble, but he still aimed the gun at Larson's big ugly bleeding nose.

Boon did not look to their leader, but seemed to be waiting for something.

"Finish him," growled Hammer.

There was no hesitation. Boon squeezed the trigger. The shot exploded as Laurie screamed. Larson twitched as the bullet passed through his forehead and then he went still, his feet lolling in opposite directions as his injured hand slipped to the ground.

Her cry and the pistol shot rang in her ears as her mind tried to reconcile such savagery.

Hammer clapped Boon on the shoulder. Boon lowered Larson's smoking pistol.

"Glad to have you back, Boon." He turned toward the men. "Larson pulled his pistols. If Boon hadn't shot him, I woulda."

Boon slid Larson's gun behind the buckle of his belt. "Who's next?"

The men shifted restlessly. Larson was the biggest among them and Boon had taken him down without suffering a scratch. The others were right to take his guns, but even without them, he'd bested their top man.

Laurie glanced about the rough-looking men. They eyed her with lust, but none stepped out to face Boon. Laurie's stomach rolled as she realized they didn't have to. Boon had not won her. He'd just won her first. If they were patient they'd still have their turn. No need to get shot over a woman.

Hammer wrapped an arm about Boon's shoulder. "He's one of us, boys."

Was he? Laurie eyed the young man. Despite the dust and stubble there was something about him that was different than the others, but perhaps this was only her mind grasping for any slim thread of hope. Then she remembered the slap and how Boon had deflected it, protecting her from harm. She watched Boon, trying to see inside his soul.

Hammer went on, as if presenting him to a family gathering, the prodigal son, returning to the flock of thieves.

"I said so the first time I laid eyes on you. Bad Boon, one of us again. Welcome home, son."

The men nodded their approval, accepting the will of their leader, all except Larson, of course. Laurie ventured a glance at the murdered man and was immediately sorry as her stomach heaved.

"Thanks." Boon's eyes narrowed and swept the gang, pausing to meet each man's cold stare. "Good to be back."

Hammer slapped him on the shoulder. "She's all yours. Have at her."

Boon didn't move.

"Well?" said Hammer.

"Not in front of them." He pointed at the others.

Hammer scowled. "What? You too shy to let them see your pecker?"

Boon said nothing.

"Maybe I'll just give her to Cal."

"I won."

Hammer glared. Boon didn't blink. Laurie found she suddenly couldn't breathe. Their leader might just as soon shoot the newest member of his group as back down. The men stood watchful, waiting for the drama to play out.

Hammer broke into a grin and then gave a laugh. "All right then, boy. Drag her off in the dark and give her a poke, but don't take too long, else I'll send the boys for their turn."

Boon came for her then, his gaze cold and dead, walking fast as if this were some burden he did not savor. She made a poor attempt at evasion and he snatched her up, dragging her to her feet as the others laughed and jeered.

She expected to see lust in his eyes, but instead he captured her gaze with one laced with what looked like regret. Laurie felt unreasonable hope welling again. What was wrong with her? He was an outlaw. She'd just watched him kill a man. *To save her,* echoed her mind. Was that the reason?

Boon laced his fingers into her long hair, now a tangled mess of pins and tendrils, what remained of the neat bun she had fashioned at her nape yesterday morning.

He drew her forward until her breasts pressed flush against the hard contours of his chest. At that intimate contact she sucked in a breath, shocked by the rush of pleasure such pressure stirred. Her eyes flashed to him, taking in the hard angles of his jaw and the eyes that seemed feral orange in the firelight.

Then he angled her head and she realized that he meant to kiss her before them all. His mouth slanted over hers. His lips were firm and his tongue hot and wet as it slid inside her mouth. She tried to struggle, but he held her firm. Her skin flashed feverish in an instant as a tremor shook her. He deepened the kiss. She moved her tongue along his, feeling the warm velvet of his mouth, tasting the sweetness of him. She leaned forward, pressing against him.

The men whistled and shouted. Laurie came back to herself with a jolt. To her horror she felt the insistent pulse of desire beating at the juncture of her legs.

Laurie tried to break free. His muscles tensed as he resisted, but then allowed her to draw back. He stared down at her with a look that was part lust and part astonishment, as if he could not comprehend her reaction any more than she could.

She whimpered as humiliation scorched her cheeks. How could she do something so low? She closed her eyes against the shame, like a child trying to disappear in plain sight. Had he not held her upper arm, she would have collapsed, for her knees now refused to hold her.

How could she be aroused by this ruthless murderer?

She struggled, but could no more escape him than a trussed turkey could escape the axe, once its head was set upon the block. As George Hammer had predicted, she had now become the show.

This is what she had feared, every waking

minute since that terrible day. Laurie fought her own shame as much as the hold of the outlaw.

She had tried to act as a proper woman, but it was just that—an act. Boon's kiss had revealed the truth. She was wanton and wicked and low, just as she feared. Had her father seen it despite her attempt to hide the truth? Had he known she was unworthy of his love? Was it her fault all along that he left them?

Laurie staggered as her knees gave way, but Boon prevented her from falling, tugging her back against him. His brow now lifted in speculation. Clearly he had not anticipated an eager partner. Laurie struggled vainly in the iron grip of the outlaw and finally let her head sink to her chest as she went still and silent. She continued to tremble as if she stood in the snow, instead of beside a fire under a warm September sky.

"Anyone pokes his nose in before I'm finished with her and I'll shoot it off."

The men glared but remained by the fire as he dragged her away. She stumbled along beside him. Behind them she heard George Hammer.

"Boon's young, boys. But young men are quick. He'll only be a minute. Where's that bottle? Cal, pass it around. Freet, Furlong, drag off the body. Throw him in the canyon for the buzzards."

Boon tugged her along, but was clearly not happy with her pace because he paused long enough to lift her into his arms before breaking into a dead run.

Laurie screamed and heard the men laughing and jeering. The night was moonless and dark as black velvet. She could see nothing as she bounced in his arms, now fearing they might fall and break their necks.

His voice rumbled through her body as he spoke. "Stop or I'll leave you behind."

What did he mean by that?

Laurie's mind dwelled again on how Boon had pulled her from the blow that George Hammer had aimed at her cheek with such finesse that the man had not even recognized what Boon had done. Her gut told her to do as he said. Still, she'd been wrong before, so wrong. Wrong about Anton, wrong about the outlaw at the station who pretended to be one of her father's men.

Laurie considered her options and decided one outlaw was better than many. One outlaw could not watch her day and night, and she might still escape.

She went limp, lying trustingly as a newborn lamb in his arms. She did not think they would get far afoot and already feared what would happen when they were caught. George Hammer had a well-earned reputation for mercilessness. One would have to be a fool not to fear him and completely insane to cross him. She looked up at the man who carried her. Which was he?

"Where are we going?"

"Quiet," he huffed and spun her up and over his shoulder as if he had some special gift for tossing young ladies about as if they were sacks of feed.

Her new position caused his shoulder to buffet her abdomen with each running stride, sending her corset stays digging into her flesh. She could scarcely draw a breath and the blood drained to her head, making it pound until she felt dizzy enough to faint.

Just as suddenly as they had begun, he stopped, grabbing her unceremoniously by the waistband of her new lavender overskirt and tugging her to her feet.

The soft nicker told her that there was a horse nearby.

"You planned this?" she asked.

He did not answer, but left her to move

in the direction of the horses. She saw them now, two large dark outlines against the canyon wall. He checked the saddle girth and the leather buckle holding the saddlebags tied across the horse's rump.

She stepped closer and saw a leather rifle scabbard tied beneath the saddle flap. The butt end of the rifle gleamed in the starlight.

There, looped over the saddle horn, was a leather cartridge belt, loaded with bullets. The twin holsters held two pistols.

Boon donned the cartridge belt, strapping it low on his hips and tying the holsters to each thigh. He stowed Larson's pistol in the boot not holding his knife. Then he turned to her and she took a step away, but not quickly enough, for he captured her about the waist.

"Up!" he said and hoisted her, then plunked her down upon the saddle, heedless of the tangle of her skirts or the complete impropriety of a woman sitting a saddle in such a fashion. An instant later, he was mounted behind her, spurring their horse. The hoofbeats told her that the second horse was strung to the saddle behind the first.

"Is this a rescue?"

"Sentry hears you, we're done."

Laurie closed her mouth as she looked around in the dark. She didn't speak again.

He made a growling sound in his throat and then wrapped his arms about her. "Hold on."

He gripped the reins, as Laurie held the saddle horn with both hands.

He had killed a man to free her. Did he want her singularly or was there a slim chance that this madness was a rescue?

They did not take off at a gallop as she would have liked, but at a steady walk along the road Laurie had traveled in the buckboard when she arrived. The night was so black that she could not see two feet before them and wondered how the horses made their way.

The journey was slow, torturously slow. Laurie strained her ears for the sound of pursuit. Boon's big body encircled hers. He wrapped one arm about her waist and dragged her into the pocket made by his chest and thighs and hunched so her corset stays impaled the soft flesh beneath her breasts.

He was warm and smelled of sweat and leather. Her chin fit under his jaw and occasionally his stubbly face scratched against her hair, further tangling the bird's nest it had become. She sat stiff with tension, trembling and breathing as quickly as she could, given the constraints of his grip and her corset.

"Shouldn't we go faster?"

"Horse breaks a leg and we're caught. Plus a walking horse is quiet. You can't hear the hoofbeats from up there." He motioned to the cliffs above them.

"I can't see," she whispered.

"Neither can the sentry, but the horses can. Now be still."

She clamped her lips down on the dozens of questions she wished to ask. *Who was he? Had her father sent him? What were his intentions? Would they make it?*

When they reached the canyon floor the sky opened up above them and the starlight glowed weakly. Rocks now loomed like outlaws hunched to spring out. They passed a scrubby piñon pine on an outcropping that so resembled a man she nearly screamed a warning.

They turned left, heading south.

"We came from that direction," she whispered.

"And that's the way they'll expect us to go. Box canyons and narrow draws this way. But I got little choice."

Behind them came the sound of gunfire.

Chapter Three

Bullets pinged off the sheer rock face of the canyon behind them.

"Firing blind in the draw, hoping to hit us," whispered Boon.

The horses set off at a trot that flowed into a lope. She craned her neck, seeing the flash of pistol fire as the sound of the riders grew louder.

Boon left the road. The horse carrying them stumbled, but recovered its footing. They slowed to a walk again and then stopped. Boon slid off the dark horse, dragging her along.

"Damned dress shines like a bedsheet."

Laurie glanced down to see it was so. The white pleated lace at her cuffs and the pale fitted lavender bodice with matching overskirt seemed to glow from within. Only the dark blue-violet fabric of her underskirt, visible below the hem of her lavender draping, vanished in the near darkness. He pushed her back between two rocks, holding the reins of both horses in one hand and her waist with the other, using his body to block hers.

She cowered behind him, clutching his vest and burying her face in the warm leather. Laurie remained motionless as the rocks, listening as the sound of hoofbeats grew closer. Gradually, the shout of riders grew more distant and the gunfire ceased.

Boon drew her out of the narrow gap. "They'll figure out which way we went pretty quick and be back again. Got an hour maybe to get ahead of them. None of them can see to track and they won't know which canyon we ducked into so we got a better than average chance of losing them in the dark." He lifted her bound hands and retrieved the knife from his boot, then sliced the ropes that had held her since her capture. She rubbed the imprints left by the cord upon her wrists with her gloved hand and flexed her numb fingers as needles of pain returned with the blood.

He turned his back, rummaging in his saddlebags. Laurie took the opportunity to run, but hindered by the restriction of the formfitting overskirt at her hips, she only reached the second horse when she heard a curse.

He was on her in an instant, capturing her about the waist, hoisting her off her feet and tucking her under his arm. Then he walked back from the horses with her draped across his hip like a naughty child.

"Ain't you got no sense? I'll tie you again." He set her on her feet and held her by the shoulders.

Even in the weak light of the stars she could make out his brow sunk low over his pale eyes as he scowled at her.

"Let me go."

"They'll catch you quicker than a treed possum. You got to mind me or we both die. Now, take off that getup."

Laurie gasped, then inched back as he advanced. Her bustle bumped into the rock face. She tried to wedge herself into the narrow gap beyond his reach. He captured her wrist easily and dragged her out. Had he done all this just to do to her what the others would have done?

"Take it off," he hissed.

"I won't," she said.

Behind them, retreating now, she could hear the men shouting Boon's name.

"They'll see you and they'll catch us," he said, as he glanced back in the direction of the riders. She had a chance then to draw his pistols and shoot him in the belly. She reached and then stopped, her fingers inches from the handle.

The riders would hear the shot and come back. What chance would she have then?

The answer was simple—none. She didn't trust Boon, but she couldn't shoot him. Laurie withdrew her hands, letting him live for now, hoping it wasn't another mistake. She glanced at his boot knife as he turned back to face her. She knew how to use a knife, but had never used one on a man.

Laurie stood mute now, pressed against the rock face.

He fumbled with the top button of her blouse.

She slapped at his hand, wishing she had shot him when she had the opportunity.

"Then *you* do it. I'll get the clothes."

Laurie stilled. *Clothes?* What was he talking about? She stood before him as he turned his back again and retrieved something from his saddlebags, then shoved it at her.

"They're boys' duds. Hurry up now."

She clutched the offering. He meant for her

to change, to increase their chances of escape. Laurie felt the air rush from her lungs and suddenly she could breathe again. Thank God she hadn't shot him.

She unfolded the bundle. Denim dungarees and a dark linsey-woolsey shirt and no underthings. She hadn't worn such garments since she was a girl, riding with her father back in San Antonio.

"Turn around," she ordered.

He did. Laurie blinked in astonishment. With a speed born of panic, she removed her dirty white cotton gloves and unfastened her jacket with trembling fingers, drawing off the basque bodice and dropping it without hesitation. Next she released the waistband of her fitted topskirts, followed by the darker underskirt, kicking them aside. The very latest thing, according to *Peterson's Ladies National Magazine,* the newer slimmer style was now a liability she could not afford. She had created the outfit, top to bottom, to impress her father with how much she had changed, at least on the outside. But the yards of fabric and lace were not worth dying for. She dropped the petticoats, then the half crinoline that helped support the skirt's draperies and the cascade of fabric of her topskirt's train. A yank released the bow fastening the horsehair bustle that had come by rail from New Hampshire.

"What's taking so long?"

The man obviously knew nothing about women's attire, thought Laurie as she unfastened the lace ruffle at her throat and released the buttons of her white blouse.

"Just a minute."

Dressed now in only her bustle, thigh-length chemise, bloomers, stockings and boots, she tried to draw on the pants but her bloomers hiked up and wadded about her waist and she could not manage to drag the Levi's over her hips.

"Hurry up," he whispered.

She pressed her lips together and tugged harder. Forced to abandon the effort, she considered riding in her bloomers, but that was out of the question. All women's bloomers were split from front to back to allow her to relieve herself without removing any of her under things or outer skirts. She blushed to think of how she once wore britches and dragged them down whenever and wherever she needed. Her mother had been quite right to object to her boyish ways. But now if she rode in this outfit, the fabric would gap if she straddled a horse and her bloomers were white as the flag of surrender.

"Laurie," Boon urged.

She began again, removing her bloomers. The trousers were tight and stiff, but she now managed to tug them on, thanks to her corset. She tucked the long chemise into the trousers. Laurie collected her gloves and stuffed them in her front pocket before hunching into the shirt. The coarse fabric brushed against her bare shoulders. She felt him staring and stilled.

Laurie glanced up and caught his eye. He looked at her with the intent gaze of a starving man. She tugged the flaps of the boys' shirt together and only then realized they did not quite cover her breasts.

"Turn around," she ordered again.

This time he shook his head in refusal. There was a new tension in him as if he was held in place by some invisible tether. Laurie's heartbeat accelerated as she recognized that she now faced a different kind of danger, the kind that came from showing a man her naked body.

"They'll be back in a moment," she warned, but she was not sure he heard her.

He stepped forward, reaching, his fingertips brushing the full round curve of the exposed tops of her breasts. She gasped and spun away, clutching her hands across her cleavage.

"I shall scream." It was an idle threat. She wouldn't, couldn't, because to scream was to draw more danger than she faced now.

But her words seemed to rouse him, for he blinked and then shook his head as if waking from a trance. He stooped to snatch up her discarded garments while Laurie tried frantically to button the shirt. She managed to get it fastened about her torso, thanks to the corset cinching her middle, but the tight fit squeezed her breasts together so they bulged at the gap in a most lurid manner.

She stared down at her white flesh, thrusting up in an open invitation, and gasped in despair. The action caused her breasts to strain against the buttons that imprisoned them. Were it not a sturdily constructed boys' shirt, she felt sure the tension would have split the seams.

Boon returned to the horses, stuffing her clothing into his saddlebags as she covered herself with her open hands, searching wildly for some other means to conceal her bosom from his view.

Boon turned. His arms dropped to his sides and his shoulders sank as if she had somehow defeated him.

"You must think I'm made of stone," he whispered.

She would have liked to point out that he was the one who chose these items for her.

"They don't fit."

"Because they told me you were a girl."

Who had told him? The hope surged, blending with the terror to steal her breath once more. Had he come just for her? Who was he? Who had sent him?

He had her wrist now, and then captured her leg, heaving her back up on the horse without a word. The dungarees stretched tight against her bottom and she feared the seam would fail. She'd never worn any garment that rubbed so intimately against her most private places. A moment later the saddle shifted under his weight as he drew up behind her.

"You're no girl," he whispered, his warm breath fanning her neck. He made it sound like a condemnation.

She felt his legs pressing the horse's sides, and they set off again, into the canyons, away from the riders and into the night.

Boon pulled Laurie flush against him. He didn't need to, but he figured if he was going to get a bullet in his back over this gal, he might just as well have the benefits of holding on to her.

He gave the horse its head, letting it pick its way along the rough trail left by the mule deer. The horse walked briskly along, but he kept them just shy of a trot. The gelding's night vision was far superior to his, but he didn't want his mount stepping into a hole and breaking a leg.

"What is your Christian name, Mr. Boon?" Laurie's whispered question sounded like a gunshot in the stillness of the night.

His lip curled in response. He wasn't like most folks with a first and last name. He had only one.

"It's just Boon."

He could feel the tension in her. What was she thinking? That he didn't want her to know his full name? If he had a last name he'd surely tell her. But he did not have one and that was all.

"I see," she whispered. But she didn't, couldn't, not without knowing where he'd come from and damned if he'd tell her that.

He turned his thoughts back to the danger they faced. The men chasing them were all drunk and they couldn't see in the dark any better than he could. Best to go easy until the moon rose, saving the horses, and then slap leather. That gave him the rest of the night with Laurie in his arms. It was the kind of temptation he never expected to face, having been told he was retrieving a girl.

Boon snuggled her against him, wondering who she was.

Why hadn't the captain told him that the girl he was rescuing was a full-grown woman? Maybe he didn't figure he owed Boon any explanation after saving his life.

When the captain took him in, Boon had thought he'd been given a second chance. Now he wasn't certain. He'd been summoned to the rooms of John Bender, the division head of the Texas Rangers. Bender and his partner, Sam Coats, had argued over whether to send him for Laurie. The captain believed in him, knew he was the best man for the job, but Coats had been against it, claiming you couldn't reform an outlaw any more than you could reform a rattlesnake. That comment had stuck to him like a cocklebur ever since. Hammer had said the same. *He's one of us, boys.*

Two men different as fire and water and both thought they knew him. Maybe they did. Were they right? Would he always be a rattlesnake, dangerous and unpredictable?

His head sank and he breathed deep of the sweet scent of Laurie's hair. Soap and lavender powder, he realized, on skin soft as a baby bunny.

Why had he let himself believe that this job was his chance to earn the captain's respect? He still thought so, or he would have ridden the other way the minute he'd left the captain. That made him worse than a fool.

Behind him the gunfire changed direction. Laurie stiffened as he cocked his head.

"They've taken the road toward the river," he whispered, as he had figured.

Laurie's breathing gradually returned to normal. He stared straight down past the waterfall of dark hair that curled across her shoulder and to her substantial bosom. He blew out a breath. One look at Laurie heated his blood and made his skin tingle as if he stood naked in the pouring rain. He tried to keep his eyes on the horse's ears as they swiveled to listen to the sounds of the night, but his mind kept throwing images of Laurie in her corset trying to button that shirt. This little gal was a temptation, the kind he'd avoided since leaving the Blue Belle.

Laurie was not what he had expected, not at all. She was all woman and a proper one at that. Her prim little coat and skirts, the upsweep of black hair that had once likely been a modest bun, and the white cotton gloves all made her seem like a lady who had been well cared for. Nothing like any woman he'd ever known.

So why had she kissed him like that?

He recalled her as he had first seen her, sitting still and watchful beside the fire, the orange flames glinting off her dark hair, giving it a red cast. She'd held her gloved hands together as if in prayer, when they were actually bound. Her stillness radiated tension and her face had pinched with worry. Her generous mouth had tipped down at the corners and her dark flashing eyes had been watchful as any cornered animal searching for escape. She'd nearly reached his horse. That showed the kind of fight she'd need if they were to get out of here. All that fit together, a brave lady captured by outlaws. What didn't fit was that kiss. In that kiss he'd experienced what she had hidden, a raw sensuality about her that burned hotter than a blacksmith's forge.

It didn't fit. That kiss, her fancy duds all bustles and lace. Who was she, the captain's woman? He was surprised at the whirlwind of anger that thought stirred.

Boon compared that first glance to the sight of her, half-dressed, lithe and winsome, standing in that cleft in the red rock struggling with the shirt he'd provided, her shoulders pale as starlight.

He wished he could look at her again, all of her this time. And he wanted to see her face in the sunlight. For now he pictured Laurie in his mind as he breathed in her scent. Her eyes were too widely set for her small oval face, he decided, too dark and too large. Both top and bottom lips were full and ripe, the top shaped like a bow and the bottom had the slightest depression at the center. He wanted to rub his thumb over that bottom lip and see her mouth open for him. Might have been a trick of the light, but her skin seemed flawless and he knew her teeth were white and straight. She was a beauty by any standard. Leave it to the Hammer to want to destroy such a woman. It made him sick.

Her face surely would be temptation enough, but Laurie had curves, full hips, a round tight backside and a full bosom, made more generous by the silly corset that pinched her middle and looked like it might break her in half like a matchstick.

He glanced back into the dark, seeing nothing but the glint of starlight on rock. With luck, Hammer's men wouldn't see their tracks until morning; by then they'd be over the rock and have a fighting chance of making the stage station where the captain would be waiting with his men.

Boon pushed the horse to a faster walk, increasing the distance between them and capture. Soon it would be light and they could ride like blue blazes. Until then the dark would hide them. The motion of the saddle rocked his hips into Laurie's bottom. He winced and shifted as his body reacted to having a beautiful woman in his arms.

Surely Captain Bender had known it would, but had sent him anyway.

Should he tell Laurie that the captain had sent him, ask what she was to him? But what if he didn't like the answer?

Fighting for her, killing for her had given him funny ideas—wrong ideas—like the notion that he had some claim over her and the feeling that he didn't want Laurie needing anybody but him. He didn't want to share her or give her over to a man old enough to be her father. What did Bender want with someone as young and sweet as Laurie? Boon knew Laurie was too good for the likes of him, but maybe she was too good for Bender, too. But Bender didn't know where to find the Hammer. Only Boon knew that. And while it was true that the Rangers could easily take the outlaws' camp, to do so would have cost Laurie her life.

Boon had gotten her out alive. Did she owe him for that? He knew that under normal circumstances she'd cross the street rather than have anything to do with someone like him. But fate had put her in his hands.

He looked at her fingers, now swathed in stained white gloves as they rested, delicate as flower petals on the saddle horn. She had high-class clothes, high-class speech and the look of someone who'd been loved and cared for her whole life.

For the course of this journey she was his. If the captain didn't like it, he should have sent one of his goddamned perfect Texas Rangers instead of a low-down murdering outlaw.

He smiled, tightening his grip upon her waist, wishing he had cut the damned corset from her. He wanted to feel the soft, warm flesh of her stomach and ribs. She was so different than the women he had known, so fresh and so full of piss and vinegar. Not beaten down or defeated, resigned or crushed by circumstance. She'd fought them and she tried to escape, twice. This was a woman who did not lie down and take what the world handed her. This was not the sort of female to give up or turn to cocaine to numb her from life's woes. She was not cynical or coarse or jaded. Fresh, vibrant and a real lady, just the opposite of those women in his past.

What he would give to have a woman like this.

What did it matter? She'd never accept the likes of him. Ladies knew enough to keep clear of rattlesnakes and outlaws.

He lifted a curling feathery wisp of hair from her neck and held it in his gloved fingers, then lifted it to his cheek. Soft as a satin ribbon, he decided. Laurie glanced back at him and then leaned away, trying to recapture her hair without snatching it from him. He released it, but her rejection stung. He knew how to make her want him. He'd learned a thing or two back there. She wouldn't be able to resist him and here she was spread out before him like a banquet. Should he take a bite? If he pleased her, would she come back for more?

Boon thought about that kiss, how Laurie had melted against him right there in front of God and everyone. Nobody had ever kissed him like that, not even Paulette. He knew some women liked his looks, the ones who preferred dangerous men. But not the good ones, not the proper ones. They stayed clear of him as if he had something catching.

Still, even a bad man could please a good woman. He could make her want him without compromising her. It would show her what he had to offer and that he was every bit as knowledgeable as Bender. Maybe if she knew, maybe she'd want to stay with him.

He snorted, disgusted at himself and the turn his thoughts had taken. He wanted her. It was the first time he'd ever really wanted a woman. There were only about a million reasons why that was a bad idea. Even so, he found himself reaching for her.

Chapter Four

They rode in silence. Laurie strained her ears for the sound of pursuit but heard nothing but their horses' hooves striking the hard-packed earth.

Boon snaked his arm about her waist again, holding her with a gentle ease she found disconcerting. Even her corset stays did not shield her from the heat and intimacy of his touch. The sensation of his warm arm, sheathed only in cotton and the leather wrist cuffs that most cowboys wore, was shocking and stimulating. To make matters worse he splayed his fingers and then drew them together absently, repeatedly, as if unaware that the tender caresses were driving her to distraction.

She straightened and wiggled in an effort

to escape the intimate contact, but her movements only served to rub her bottom into the cleft of his lap. Laurie stilled at the thrill of excitement that shot through her. She heard him draw breath.

"You're driving me crazy, Laurie-gal."

Even his voice disturbed her, making her insides all liquid and warm. Still, she denied what was happening between them. "I'm doing no such thing."

"You are. Ripe as a summer peach. Makes me want to take a bite."

He nuzzled her neck as the horses walked steadily on. The sensation was the most erotic of her life. His warm lips moistened her skin and his hot breath dried it again, leaving her flesh tingling and sensitive. Boon rubbed his stubbled cheek against her downy one and hummed. The deep, low rumble vibrated through her like distant thunder. Laurie drew a sharp breath, trying to control the urge to lift her gloved hand and stroke the strong line of his jaw. She shouldn't, couldn't encourage him, but neither did she try to stop him. Instead she clutched the saddle horn with greater ferocity as she leaned back against him.

Boon's lips pressed to her ear and she

melted. If not for the corset she'd be puddled around him like butter left in a sunny window.

His whisper ruffled the hair curling about her cheek.

"That kiss. Can't get it out of my head. You sure don't kiss like a lady."

Laurie's head sank as she realized how quickly he had seen through her facade. Was that why he was stroking her; did he suspect the truth? It was a terror of hers, that men could tell, just by looking, what she had done.

"Laurie, why?" His words were a whispered caress, a hot demand brushing against her ear. "Why'd you do it?"

How could she answer a question like that when she knew such behavior was inexcusable?

"I don't know." Her voice had become a strangled thing that she hardly recognized as her own.

"Likely you don't. But I do."

She surrendered to the urge to touch him by laying her head against his broad shoulder and turning away from him so he could not see the hot flush of shame burning her cheeks. Laurie tried not to cry. She was all a jumble inside, wanting one thing and needing quite another. She wanted him to leave her be, wanted to tell him to stop touching her. But her body urged her to rub up against him like a cat demanding to be stroked.

He lifted his hand. When had he removed his glove? Boon trailed his fingers along the column of her neck as if she had intentionally offered the bare flesh just to him. Slowly the caresses reached her throat.

Her breasts felt achy, as if they swelled with the wanting he stirred. A mutiny, she realized, her desires commandeering her rational mind. Now instead of inching away, she pressed back, closing her eyes at the shame and the delight. What was he doing to her and why did she need it so badly?

The desire to feel his hands upon her breasts grew until she had to clamp her teeth together to keep from begging him to touch her. She'd staunched her words, but not the soft moan that rumbled in the back of her throat.

Had he heard it? He nuzzled her neck, lips dropping hot kisses on scorched skin.

Humiliation burned her as the cursed trousers rubbed against the sensitive flesh at her cleft with each rocking step of the horse. The rhythmic bob of the saddle beneath them and the feathery caress of Boon's experienced fingers set off a whirlwind within her.

All about them the stars wheeled, but down here on the canyon floor, darkness cloaked their passing.

She whimpered, but he did not release her. Instead, he nuzzled her ear, taking her soft lobe in his mouth and sucking. She shivered with delight.

His hand remained splayed over her collarbone, maddeningly high. If only he would cup her breast with those big callused hands.

"What do you want, Laurie-gal?"

But she couldn't say what she wanted aloud, for she didn't know. And if she did know, she felt certain it was wicked and wrong to want it.

"Tell me," he urged.

"No," she whispered, shocked at the breathy quality of her voice.

He chuckled, his chest rumbling behind her like a kettle drum. "No one will know," he whispered. "Be our secret."

Secret, yes, just another secret.

He had woven some spell over her, made her body turn against her, until she longed for his touch, ached for it. He slid one hand down, cupping her breast, kneading the sensitive flesh and bringing her nipple to a tight throbbing bud of need. He pinched it gently between his thumb and forefinger. Oh, he was making it worse. Now she burned and the aching sensitivity increased with each wonderful, masterful touch. Deep inside her core, she felt her body quicken and then came the liquid heat where she touched the saddle. How did he know to do these things, how did he know her body better than she did?

She could not catch her breath and she felt feverish and weak. Now he had both hands upon her breasts, pressing her against his body, kissing her neck and ear. Each time his lips touched hers, he sent shivering tremors through her, like tiny earthquakes. Her head fell back against his chest and she lifted her chin offering her lips, longing to feel his kiss once more.

His mouth moved over hers, their kiss deep and long. Laurie trembled as his hands snaked down over her twitching belly and to the rivet that held her jeans. Though the fit was tight on her hips, the waist gaped and he had no trouble releasing the rivets. His fingers delved into her thick curls, burrowing deeper, closer to her most private places. She shifted in a poor effort to evade his touch but only succeeded in helping him reach his goal. He found her cleft, sliding his fingers over her slippery flesh. She gasped in shock and need. This was wrong.

She knew it, yet she said nothing to stop him. But this time, she wanted the touch, craved it.

"Lean back…that's it. Let me touch you."

She did as he bid her, rolling her hips so he could stroke her needy nub of flesh, and was rewarded instantly with a curling, building tension which began where he caressed her and crept outward. Her body flexed as she rocked against his stroking fingers, beginning a slow rolling rhythm.

"That's it. Nice and slow."

Something was happening. She couldn't move slowly any longer. The urge to thrust overcame her and she began to rock her hips in a way that was new, yet familiar. She climbed toward a new goal as her body moved in ways she did not recognize. She lifted her arms and locked them about his neck, pulling, arching. His mouth moved to the shell of her ear.

She couldn't get enough air and feared she might faint. What was happening to her? With a suddenness that shocked her, the tension, which had built with each slow rocking motion of the man's hands and the saddle, released in a tumbling waterfall of pleasure, flowing outward from his masterful fingers, rippling in all directions with a force that caused her to arch as if he had stabbed her in the back. She tried to scream, but his mouth covered hers, silencing her cry as she clung, wrapping her arms around his neck, allowing his tongue to plunder her mouth.

The waves of pleasure receded, replaced by a lethargy. Laurie's arms slipped from about his neck and she collapsed against him. Gradually she came back to herself. She lay quivering, enfolded in his strong arms, his chin now resting familiar upon the top of her head.

Laurie blinked, becoming aware by slow degrees. What in the world was that?

She looked about.

They still rode slowly along, the horse picking his way in near silence. Their pursuers had vanished in the shroud of darkness. And Boon still hugged her close, as if she belonged to him, one arm about her waist and the other cupping her at the juncture of her thighs in some vulgar mockery of an embrace. Laurie glanced at herself, seeing his dark hand thrust lewdly down her open trousers. When had he unbuttoned her shirt? How had he managed to get the shirt open and her camisole unlaced?

She'd acted just like a prostitute, taking her pleasure, rubbing up against him like a mare in heat. She lifted her hands to cover her burning eyes. It didn't help. She still wanted to cry.

"Feeling better?" he asked, as if it were perfectly natural to ride with her blouse open and his hand down her pants.

She gave a little cry of dismay.

"Laurie?" His voice now held caution.

She writhed, nearly falling from the horse.

He withdrew his hand and grasped her, hauling her back before himself. "What are you doing?"

"How could I allow you?" she whispered, pressing her hands to cover her eyes.

"Just natural, I guess."

She did not know how to respond to such an answer. She was mortified. He was a complete stranger, yet she had not made the slightest effort to prevent him from touching her. The terrible truth was that she had welcomed it.

"Laurie?" His voice had lost the easy confidence of a moment ago as uncertainty crept in.

If she could have sunk to the canyon floor and died she surely would have. Had they not been on horseback, she was certain that he would have taken her, just as she deserved, on the ground, like an animal.

As she fumbled with her camisole and fastened the rivets of the hated trousers, the tears came.

"You've shamed me." Her head hung as she

tugged at the shirt, still unable to completely button it.

"Shamed?"

How dare he sound surprised? She wanted to slap him; instead she dashed away the tears coursing down her cheeks.

"I just tried to, well, I thought you wanted to."

Laurie held both hands over her mouth, feeling dizzy and sick.

"I don't understand this." Her voice had that high wavering quality that told her she was perilously close to sobbing.

"Just trying to bring you ease."

The casualness of his reply shocked her speechless.

"Thought it might take your mind off your troubles for a little while."

"No! You've only added to them. Oh," she cried, "but I didn't even try to stop you."

"You're human."

"My display was disgraceful!"

"Beautiful," he whispered.

She paused trying to decide if he was mocking her but could not tell.

"Women got needs, too, you know."

"Needs? No. A lady most certainly does not have needs."

He gave a snort. "Well, you could be right about that, 'cause I never been with a lady before." He leaned close and nibbled the shell of her ear. "But I like it."

She slapped at him. "Stop that. Don't touch me."

"That'd be some trick, riding double. Guess I'll touch you if I like."

Laurie hung her head. She was a fraud and a fake, just as she'd feared. She wasn't fit for decent society. No wonder she'd failed to attract a decent man. How could she convince a respectable gentleman that she would make him a proper wife if she allowed herself to be treated in such a low manner?

Sweet lord, even an outlaw could tell the difference. She was no lady. Had not been since… No, she would not think on that. Only two people on earth knew and she'd never tell. She had spent the past years trying to pretend that episode had never happened. Did her father know? Was that why he had left them?

All this time she had tried so hard to convince herself that her troubles were behind her and that, if she could only convince her parents to reconcile, if they would end this separation and remarry, then she could set aside the stigma of divorce. She'd nearly convinced herself that it was their actions, not hers, that kept her from a decent match. But in her heart she knew the truth. No decent man would have her because she was ruined.

The trouble was not her parents' divorce, but the flaw that she could not hide. What if every man who looked at her could already tell what had happened to her?

Laurie felt cold that cut bone deep as she admitted to herself that the problem all along had been herself. She wouldn't let a man near her and that was a fact.

She closed her eyes and prayed. *Please, God, forgive me my trespasses. Don't let me fall for an outlaw and live a wicked life. Please let me wake up and find this is all just a nightmare.*

Hot tears splashed down her cheeks.

Nothing had changed and somehow this outlaw had seen right through her and into her wanton heart. The past four years had been nothing but a lie.

Laurie opened her eyes and noticed the ghostly pale landscape, made visible by the slip of a moon, nearly in its quarter, rising silver above the canyon rim. She could no longer see the stars. Laurie stiffened at the significance. If she could see about them, the outlaws could, as well.

"Can you sit a horse solo?" he asked.

"Ladies don't ride astride." She scrubbed her hands over her face, wiping away the tears with the grit.

The truth was her father had taught her when she was a girl. She had loved the freedom of galloping over the countryside. But that was before she understood how unseemly such behavior was. Ladies did not ride; they sat in carriages. But riding meant escape from Hammer and it meant distance from Boon. She needed that more than she needed to protect her crumpled dignity. Besides, he'd already discovered what kind of a woman she really was.

"Is that a no?"

She shook her head, sending her lopsided bun further into decline.

Boon reined in. He dismounted then clasped her waist and pulled her down, his big hands sliding under her shirt and against the barrier of her corset. He set her on her feet but did not let go.

"You know better than to try and run?"

She kept her head lowered, unable to bear meeting his eyes after what they had done together. But she could not control the trembling and he noted it.

"Laurie?" His voice held a new caution.

He clasped her chin in his hand and lifted. She kept her eyes downcast, as another tear rolled down her face.

His voice filled with incredulity. "You crying?"

"No."

"Because of what we done?"

"No, I said!" Laurie pressed her lips together and glared, daring him to call her a liar, even with the evidence right there on her cheek.

He released her, stepping back and resting his hands on his hips just above his guns. She wondered what he had expected her to do, thank him?

Suddenly the shame boiled up, like scalding milk topping the pot and pouring over the sides. She seethed with fury, not for his touching her but for his so easily discovering that he *could* touch her.

"How did you know?" she demanded, her words as hot as her tears.

He tucked his chin and looked uneasy. "What?"

"How could you tell just by looking?" Her

words were a shouted whisper, hoarse and feral.

He shifted and stepped back as if preparing to run from the madwoman.

"Tell what?"

"Somehow you saw through me, Boon. I want to know just what I said or did that told you I'm not the lady I appear to be. Was it the kiss?"

He nodded, his brow tented and ears pinned back now, like a dog trying to comprehend.

"Nobody ever kissed me like that," he admitted. "Maybe I shouldn't have done what I done, but I didn't know…" His words fell off.

"Didn't know what? That I wouldn't stop you?" Laurie gripped her hair at each side of her head, trying to keep from screaming. No wonder she couldn't find a husband. It wasn't her mother's divorce, it was her. It was obvious to any man that she wasn't a lady.

"I was going to say that I didn't know no other way to comfort you. I ain't been around ladies much, or at all, really."

"Well, let me edify you, then. That is *not* the way you comfort a lady!" she shouted, further proving she was incapable of civil behavior. Laurie whirled away, took three steps and then covered her face with her dirty gloves and sobbed.

He didn't approach her or try to comfort her. Finally when her sobs had turned into a racking, shuddering breath, he spoke, his voice low.

"Laurie, I'm sorry for what I done. I never meant to grieve you. But we gotta ride or Hammer will catch us."

She turned to face him, her eyes burning and her chin trembling.

"If you can't sit a saddle, we can ride double, but we gotta switch horses."

She glared at him for forcing her to admit yet another shortcoming.

"I can ride astride."

He pushed back the brim of his hat to stare at her, his face silvery in the moonlight. She wondered what he could see of her.

"I can!" she insisted. "And I can shoot and rope and tell the direction just by moonlight. North." She pointed her gloved hand.

His brows rose as he considered her a moment. "All right then."

He offered his hands as a mounting block. She stalked over to him.

"Give me your kerchief." She held out her hand, demanding it.

He narrowed his eyes and then did as she asked, untying the wide strip of pale fabric.

She tied it about her neck and then tucked it into her camisole as if it were a lace collar. Having removed the sight of her décolletage from his sight, she buttoned up the shirt as best she could and tugged it straight.

"Ready?" he asked, offering his clasped hands again.

She refused his offered help, lifted a foot to the stirrup and swung into the saddle, then stared down her nose at him.

Boon reset his hat and stared a moment longer, then stalked away.

Laurie lifted the reins and remembered all her father had taught her. Why was it easier to remember than to forget?

Boon returned a moment later with a lead line that he fastened between her horse's bridle and the rear rigging dee of his saddle. Clearly he did not believe she could ride or did not trust her to ride in the same direction as he did.

Did he think she'd run?

Once mounted, he twisted in the saddle to look back at her. "Don't fall off. If you feel sleepy give a holler. We'll be riding faster as the light comes up. With luck we'll find another way out of these canyons."

He didn't have an escape route planned? Laurie felt the anxiety prickling in her belly like a stalk of nettles. She glanced back at the way they had come and could see their horses' tracks in the sand. The shroud of darkness was dissolving like mist, retreating against the rising moon, and the outlaws were back there, coming for them.

Her father had hanged George Hammer's little brother. That meant Hammer wouldn't stop until he caught them.

Did Boon know who her father was?

Was he rescuing her, or perhaps her father had offered some bounty and he was trying to collect the ransom himself. She hoped he hadn't taken her with something else in mind.

Laurie wondered if knowing that her father was John Bender, the Indian fighter and renowned Texas Ranger, would help her or hurt her. Boon was an outlaw. He might not want to save the daughter of a man sworn to hunt him down and kill him.

Laurie decided to keep silent until she knew more about this man and his intentions. Until then she'd look for a chance to escape.

"Hold on," Boon called and then kicked them to a gallop.

Laurie gritted her teeth and lifted the reins. If they managed to escape, would her father even want her back?

Chapter Five

They'd ridden through the night past the silvery tufts of sage grass and squatty juniper that somehow survived growing in nothing but dry gravel. Boon followed the channel that had cut this canyon, up a wide dry wash that could fill in a moment with runoff from a storm upstream. When they veered off the main channel, he hoped he'd chosen wisely and that this finger would bring them back to the surface without having to abandon their horses. Boon had stopped only to brush away their tracks back as far as the last draw. Hammer knew this territory, but the steady wind eroded their tracks and only the fading quarter moon marked their passing, allowing them greater speed.

He glanced back at Laurie, motionless, her chin on her chest and her posture defeated. She'd stopped her sniffling, but her tears still tore into him worse than cat-claw thorns.

If there was any doubt in anyone's mind about his suitability as a Texas Ranger, Boon's actions had settled the matter. What he'd read as Laurie's consent turned out to be only her inexperience. What he'd thought was a gift, a way to distract and comfort, ended up being neither. Paulette had told him this was what all women wanted. But then why did it make Laurie cry? She'd seemed to enjoy it at the time and it sickened him to think that he had taken advantage of her, when he'd only meant to give her pleasure.

Paulette, a new arrival to the Blue Belle, had taught him that this was how you gave a woman her release and that there was no danger of unwanted children this way. Then why was Laurie so grieved?

The truth settled heavy in his chest.

He'd taken advantage of a woman in his care, something he knew a Ranger would never do. He was no better than the animals on their trail, just another brutal outlaw who used women for sport. He thought of his mother and his shoulders sank another inch.

He glanced toward the sky again, certain this time that the stars had begun to vanish. Dawn was coming and with it the desert heat. Something rustled in the brush. Likely a porcupine or armadillo, he thought, continuing on. The cry from behind him brought him about in his saddle. Laurie gripped the saddle horn with both hands and was hauling herself back into the saddle seat.

He turned his mount.

"I fell asleep," she admitted.

Boon nodded, reaching for her.

"What are you doing?"

He pulled her from the saddle and settled her in front of him.

"I'm awake now. No need to trouble yourself."

"If you fall, you might bust something. You rest a bit."

She wiggled her hips to settle before him and he gritted his teeth against the physical reaction of his body to hers. He'd not touch her again, he vowed. Laurie stilled, suddenly motionless as a rabbit before a fox.

"Where are you taking me?" she asked.

His first thought was Mexico, but he knew he couldn't just ride off with her. That would be wrong. Then why did his mind fix on the notion like a feather caught in tar?

He wrapped one arm about her waist and nudged the horse to a fast walk.

"I'm bringing you home, Laurie."

"You are?" Her voice echoed with astonishment. Could she not even conceive of someone like him doing the decent thing?

"That's right."

"To my father?"

He didn't know her father or his connection to the captain.

"I suppose. I'm here on orders from the Texas Rangers under Captain John Bender. You heard of him?" He puffed up a little when he said it, proud to be associated with Bender, even if the association was only temporary. He wondered again if he could make it permanent. Maybe the captain would see, when he brought Laurie home safe, that he'd be a welcome addition to Bender's division.

Laurie turned and stared up at him, her expression confused.

She clarified. "Captain John Bender, famous lawman, legendary Indian fighter, that John Bender?"

"The same."

Boon lifted his chin a notch, hoping she was impressed.

"He sent you?"

Uncertainty flickered down low in his belly, but he nodded.

"I just said so." Had she heard of him or not?

"*That* John Bender is my father."

Boon swayed, and had it not been for the saddle cantle behind him he'd have likely dropped over backward. He felt as if she'd punched him in the stomach, would have preferred it in fact. She still stared at him, half-turned in the saddle, one brow lifted in speculation.

"You didn't know," she said.

He shook his head in answer as the truth descended upon him like a cloud of locusts from a blue sky. She wasn't Bender's woman. This was his child and Boon had done things to Laurie to which a father would surely take offense. He'd made the captain's daughter cry.

Boon's little dream of joining the Rangers burst like a soap bubble in the sun, lost forever.

He'd never join that division of elite fighters, earn the respect of the captain or be anything other than what he was. Reality blinded him. Coats was right. Once a snake, always a snake.

If he was smart he'd drop her at the stage station and head in the opposite direction as fast as he could ride. If he were lucky he might make Mexico before the Rangers ran him to ground. Boon pulled to a halt and dismounted, dropping the reins and walking away from the horses. His stride was quick at first then slowed until he stood with both hands laced behind his neck, his elbows stretched wide as he looked to the heavens.

The captain's words came back to him. *I don't care. I want her back.*

His partner had told Bender it was a mistake. Now Boon understood what *it* was—it was him. *He* was the mistake. The captain hadn't sent him because he was the best man for the job or even his first choice. Boon was his *only* choice and he hadn't expected that the outlaw would treat his daughter honorably or he would have told him who Laurie was. Instead, the captain had kept it secret. Boon replayed the conversation he'd overheard in his mind. It all made sense now. Bender wanted his daughter back so badly he had been willing to do anything, even allow a known outlaw to defile his little girl. The captain loved

Laurie enough to let it happen just to get her back alive.

The realization hit him right in the gut. Bender didn't trust him. He'd sent Boon because he'd had no other choice.

Boon folded at the middle as his empty stomach pitched.

Bands of pink and orange light reached across the eastern sky. Morning had found them, still in the box canyon.

Laurie watched her rescuer with cautious eyes. Boon looked like a prisoner giving himself up and now he looked as if he were going to be sick.

His horse did not know what to make of this abandonment and so the chestnut gelding glanced toward Laurie, showing her the small white stripe down his face, and then took a few steps in Boon's direction, snorting loudly. This caused Laurie's bay to prick its ears, regarding the man who stood with his back to them all.

He did not turn, but remained still as the stone walls while the first rays of light painted the canyon rim a brilliant red.

Laurie felt as wrung out as damp laundry from her ordeal, and now this man, her rescuer, had made her feel things she did not know were possible. Surely what they had done must be sinful and wrong. It hurt to know that he had seen through her like glass. Had her fancy dresses and proper bonnets only made her a joke to everyone back in Fort Worth?

Boon seemed befuddled that she was the daughter of John Bender. His reaction worried her. Now that he knew, would he leave her?

"Boon?" she said, trying to keep the fear from creeping into her voice.

She untied the rope joining their horses and then glanced back to Boon.

He removed his gray felt hat and threw it with great force toward the ground. When it landed before him, he kicked it. His hair was not brown, she could see now in the breaking dawn that his highlights were very definitely a honey-blond and shaggy.

As she watched, his shoulders rose and fell in a heavy sigh. He retrieved his hat and dusted it off before returning it to his head.

He spun on her, turning like a gunslinger about to draw, but all he aimed at her was his cold stare.

"Your father?" he asked, the incredulity of his voice now settling to dismay.

She nodded.

"You'd think he would have mentioned

that." Boon returned to collect the reins of the gelding. "Might as well get you down. Have to switch horses anyway."

His hands splayed her waist, lifting her up naturally as if she belonged to him. He held her easily, controlling her descent until she stood before him, gazing up into his troubled eyes, a clear cobalt-blue, she realized. His hair curled playfully at his neck beneath that wide-brimmed hat. The stiffness of her muscles, the bone weariness and the worry all dissolved like a shallow puddle in the summer sun as he held her with his gaze.

She felt a zap of energy. A little pop of attraction, one to the other. It was happening again, that need to move closer, to lift her hand to touch his face. Laurie could not look away.

He stared down at her, hands still holding her waist. His expression troubled.

"I'd have done differently had I known," he whispered.

"Because you're afraid of my father." It wasn't a question. Most men were afraid of John Bender, and Boon had more cause than many. Hammer said he was one of his gang, but Boon said he was sent by her father. What was the truth?

He shook his head in slow deliberation.

"Because I respect him. Would have liked to earn his respect, as well. Now…" He shrugged hopelessly.

Laurie wanted to tell him that it would be easier to sprout wings and fly than earn her father's respect. Hadn't she tried and failed her entire adult life? As soon as she put away her britches, he had drifted away. What was it about John Bender that garnered the instant esteem of one and all? And why did he take such devotion completely for granted?

"I promised I'd bring you to him and I aim to do just that or die trying."

Die…yes, Laurie realized, that was still a very real possibility. He had double-crossed a dangerous outlaw and that would make him a marked man. George Hammer would never forgive such a betrayal.

"What if they catch us?" she asked.

He regarded her with a long silent stare. "I'll do all I can to protect you."

"Don't let them capture me again."

His dark brows lifted in an unspoken question and she held his gaze. His expression told her he understood what she asked. Boon nodded his acceptance of this new burden, shouldering it with the rest.

"You promise?" she asked.

"They won't take you alive."

A flicker of relief danced inside her with the gratitude. "Thank you."

His piercing blue eyes pinned her as his gaze traveled over her face.

"You got a shiner," he said, lifting a finger to gently brush her left cheek.

Laurie absorbed the tingle of awareness caused by the feathery touch. She clasped a hand over the bruise that Hammer had given her, noting that her cheek felt puffy beneath her fingertips.

"Is it bad?" she asked, lowering her hand and angling her cheek to give him a better look.

He pursed his lips. "Seen worse."

She was suddenly anxious to be gone. Laurie glanced back at the way they'd come, seeing nothing but the scrappy juniper and tuffs of broomweed that dotted the dry, rocky canyon floor. Boon's hands slipped away, the spell between them broken once more.

He moved to her horse, lifting the rope that had connected their mounts and then staring at the end. He glanced back at her with a knowing look and a smile that showed a kind of begrudging respect. Then he dropped the line and retrieved a canteen from the saddlebags on the second horse and offered it to her. "Just warm water," he said.

She drank greedily, then realized there might not be more anytime soon and forced herself to stop, returning the canteen. Boon poured some into his hat and offered it to his horse, then repeated the process for the bay who slurped it all up. Boon took no water himself.

He was studying their surroundings now. She watched him as he turned in a slow circle. The walls looked impossibly high, a prison, she realized. The sun rays crept down the rim of the canyon, sending light across the opposite bank of rock and painting it orange.

Boon motioned to her horse. "Up you go."

He bent and offered his clasped hands to boost her into the saddle, then recalled his last attempt and straightened, lifting a hand toward the horse. Laurie grabbed the horn in two hands and swung up.

Boon gathered her reins and offered them to her. She collected them neatly in one hand, shortening the length to bring her horse's head up.

"Seems you've ridden a fair piece."

"My father taught me," she said.

Boon lifted the lead rope from the ground

and began coiling it, replacing the looped line to his saddle. His actions said he trusted her not to run. Their eyes met and she gave him a smile of gratitude.

"How did you meet my father?"

He glanced back the way they had come again and then to her. "Caught us robbing a string of horses. Bad timing on Hammer's part. One of your father's men shot my horse out from under me at two hundred yards. Hell of a shot."

"That'd be my father's partner."

"Coats? Might be. My horse pinned my leg. Hammer and his men left me to hang, maybe hoping finding me would slow the Rangers down, which it did. But your father surprised me. He didn't string me up, as expected. He listened to my story and gave me a second chance."

That didn't sound like her father. She wondered what he had seen in Boon to make him take such an unexpected step. Surely he was not captivated by his features or mesmerized by his startling blue eyes. Boon's eyebrows tented as he puzzled over her long steady stare.

"Why were you riding with outlaws?"

Boon's eyes slid away as if he could no longer meet her gaze. His eyes narrowed on her as if blaming her for asking such a question.

"'Cause I *am* an outlaw."

Laurie's stomach dropped. Just what kind of a man had her father sent for her? She'd seen Boon kill Larson over her. She knew he was a brutally effective fighter and completely without mercy. But she had held out hope that he was not like those others.

"But…"

He cut her off. "I'm a killer, Laurie. Don't forget it."

Why had she allowed herself the delusion of believing he was different? And why had she held hope? Because he had such handsome features. He did not look like a desperado. But that was not all. It was also because of what she felt when he touched her. How could an outlaw make her feel like that?

He broke her silent appraisal by motioning his head toward the horses.

"You ready?" he asked.

He looked up at her, his eyes now hard and angry, his lips pressed together and his chin lifted as if waiting for her condemnation.

She wanted to ask him what had happened to cause him to fall in with such men. Had it been an accident or was there a billet in each sheriff's office with his name upon it? Did her father have his wanted poster even now?

But she did not ask and she realized that it was because she did not want to know, did not want her pretty illusion of him to have to be bothered with the truth.

Boon was a thief and a murderer. She tried to reconcile his handsome face, engaging eyes and earnest expression with what she now knew. She wanted to tell him that he just didn't look like a killer. But her own experience proved the fallacy of that train of thinking. His youth and good looks did not preclude him being a dangerous man. She immediately thought of the baby-faced William McCarty, or Billy the Kid as he was now known.

Couldn't Boon's killing have been an accident? She longed to ask, feared the answer and said nothing.

Boon broke eye contact and checked his horse's saddle. When he spoke it was over his shoulder, not looking at her.

"Gonna be riding fast now. So will they, looking for sign. Keep hold of the saddle horn on these steep grades. All right?"

In answer she lifted the reins confidently in one hand, eyeing him coolly as he quirked a brow.

"How far back to you suppose they are?"

"Not sure. Might have lost them. But Hammer wants you real bad, so he won't quit."

He spun away, gracefully sweeping up into the saddle with a jump and roll that did not require use of the stirrup. Laurie blinked in astonishment at the athleticism of the man.

For the rest of the morning, Laurie held her seat as her teeth knocked together and her bottom bounced upon the unforgiving leather seat. She realized she was no longer that spry little girl in a saddle the size of a rocking chair, riding along on flat and familiar territory. However did her father spend so much of his life in the saddle?

When the sun was directly above them, Laurie suffered from a great thirst, but each time she thought to ask him for water, she recalled that he had taken none and somehow managed to keep her mouth closed.

He was risking his life to save hers. The least she could do was not hinder his efforts.

Likely it was the jarring gait that kept her from noticing the increasing greenery about them. It was not until the appearance of stringy cottonwood that she became cognizant of what was happening.

It was only a short time later that the trickle

of water became evident beside the trail. Boon forged on, resisting his horses' attempt to move to water until they were well up the creek and the water was flowing fast. Only then did he pause to allow the animals to drink their fill.

The horses slurped and blew, pawing at the water. Laurie felt sorry for the horses; their sides were soapy with frothing sweat and their saddle blankets soaked through.

Laurie looked longingly at the muddy water.

"It's not safe to drink," he said. "I'd feel happier if it were running faster."

She nodded her understanding, but still eyed the enticing stream.

He offered her the canteen.

Laurie lifted a hand in refusal. "You first."

Boon shook his head pressing the canteen into her hands. "Nobody in this world cares if I come back. It's you everybody is after."

"Then I won't drink, either." Laurie held out the canteen.

Boon scowled. He twisted off the top and took a long swallow before handing it back.

"You're stubborn," he said.

She didn't deny it. It was what had kept her from realizing her mother was right all along. Little girls need to follow rules or there are consequences—terrible consequences.

"Likely that kept you alive back there."

Laurie drank, being careful not to drain the last, though she wanted to. The water was hot now, but it satisfied her thirst.

"I knew my father was coming for me. I just needed to stay alive until he did. I wasn't afraid of dying so much as..." Her words fell off. How could she say aloud what she most feared?

"How did they find you?"

"Hammer said they intercepted my letter. They were waiting for me. Knew I was coming. At the time I was disheartened that my father did not respond to my communiqué but still resolute. I walked right into the lion's den."

"Likely it went by overland stage." He sounded resigned.

"Yes, Hammer said that one of his men robbed a mail stage."

He released a weary breath. "My stage. I was riding shotgun on C. Bain & Company when Hammer's men robbed it. That was about a month ago. They stole the lot. Your letter with the rest."

Laurie's breath caught as she calculated the days. The timing would have been right.

She recalled her arrival again, seeing it now

from a new perspective and recognizing her mistakes. "I knew something was wrong the moment I first set eyes on Mr. Katz." Her internal alarm system had sounded but she had been too distracted by her father's absence to pay heed. "But he showed me his Texas star and I climbed into the dilapidated buckboard I thought my father had sent for me. I was so stupid. I just climbed up and sat right next to him. I was more concerned about staining my new lilac overskirts and wondering why my father hadn't come in person to listen to my own doubts."

Boon didn't judge. He didn't roll his eyes at her stupidity or look away in disgust. He just listened with an intent, open expression that she appreciated.

"I thought the urgency of my letter would affect him and was peeved at his absence." She was boggled by her own naiveté.

"Urgency?"

"Yes, you see, my father and mother have been…" She hesitated to speak of family business.

"Laurie, I ain't a gossip. And besides, who am I going to tell? My horse?"

She looked about at the horse in question wondering what secrets the animal knew about

Boon and finding herself much more curious than was proper.

"My mother left my father when I was fourteen. I don't know why exactly. They had words. I do know it had something to do with me. My mother didn't like my wearing britches and riding out alone."

"That riding kept us ahead of Hammer."

"My mother also didn't think it proper that I rope and shoot and brand cattle. I've even helped birth calves. When she discovered that she was livid."

"I'd imagine so." Boon rubbed the back of his neck. "Never seen a female do those things."

"It was all they ever fought about. My father telling her to let me be. My mother insisting I was too old for britches." Her mother had been right about everything. Laurie had gotten herself into trouble, just as her mother had predicted, only not the kind that she'd expected. When Laurie had gone to her afterward her mother knew something was wrong, but she never asked. It was as if she didn't want to know. But she started packing that very day. "In any case, I put away my boyish things and went with my mother to Fort Worth. She found a school for young ladies in Dallas." She held her arms out to illustrate the changes then realized she wore britches again and looked very much like the little wild child she had once been. Her shoulders slumped. "Father never came to visit. At first he sent letters. But lately…"

The lump prevented her from saying more. Was that the real reason she came back? Was her mother's announcement just the excuse she needed to see him again?

"Laurie?" Boon's voice held a note of caution. The gentle touch of his hand on her shoulder radiated concern.

"They divorced." She spoke the words at a whisper as the self-reproach clung to her like wet clay. It was her fault. She knew it, but did her father? "Now she is planning to remarry."

His hand slipped away and she glanced up, meeting his quiet stare. "You thought he should know?"

"Exactly." She lowered her chin. "When I told my mother that very thing she said, 'Laurie, honey, that man hasn't had a passing interest in anything I've done for over ten years. What makes you think this would be any different?' But I *did* think this would be different. We had words and that's why I was distracted. I was going to tell him that their divorce hurt my chances of marrying a respectable man and that they should reconcile for my sake."

His face now turned stormy. "You're ashamed of your mom because she's divorced?"

Laurie nodded.

He snorted. "There's worse things."

"Well, if there are, I don't know what. We aren't invited to social occasions and I've seen more than one young man turned away from me."

She secretly believed it was her inability to be alone with a man without breaking into a cold sweat that was more the issue. She glanced at Boon. She wasn't sweating now. What was it about him that made her feel safe?

He was frowning. "That why you ain't hitched? Because of your mom and dad? I'd think your looks would make a man forget anything else."

His comment made her feel warm inside. Did he really think she was pretty? "In some circles a woman's lineage is more important."

He shook his head in confusion or possibly disgust. "World's gone crazy."

"Now Mother is going to marry the owner of a string of liveries in Austin. I don't want to move to Austin and I don't want another father. I want *my* father." She reminded herself belatedly that a lady does not raise her voice.

"You're grown, Laurie. I guess you can do as you like."

She gasped at that. "Yes, what I like. Taking the train to San Antonio, for example. I thought that was a fine idea. I was going to sweep in and fix everything. As soon as my father heard his wife was planning to remarry, he'd jump on his horse and ride after her. Only instead I was waylaid by an outlaw."

"Which one took you?"

She knew what he asked. Her captor had a sallow complexion a dirty neck and a twitchy manner.

"Katz," she whispered, and could not repress the shiver.

"Did he touch you?" His voice went low and hard. It stopped her breathing for a moment. The look in his eyes gave no reassurance.

She knew what he meant and couldn't keep from giving a mad shaking of her head that pulled loose another strand of hair from the disaster her coiffure had become.

"No. No, he didn't. He showed me a Ranger's star and told me he'd been sent by my father." She glanced at the water, watching a yellow leaf swirl as it flowed downstream. "I remember thinking that Rangers used to have better manners. I knew something was wrong, but I kept thinking that maybe my father really would let my mother go if he didn't even care enough to meet me at the station. That he wasn't really, secretly, still madly in love with Mother. That he wasn't keeping his distance only to protect us from his many enemies. And he had not been secretly checking on my progress through his connections in town. I was so self-absorbed I didn't even notice Katz driving me out of town.

"When I did notice, really looked, I started asking questions. When had my father given up his rooms at the hotel? How much farther? And then I realized what had bothered me from the start."

Boon lifted his chin a peg urging her to continue.

"Why had he tucked his star in his pocket? All the Texas Rangers I knew wore their star pinned to their hat or coat. They didn't hide them in their clothing. Then I felt ill, dizzy, too, as if I were looking down from the crest of a mesa. If he wasn't a Texas Ranger, who was I riding with? For he wasn't who he purported himself to be."

"So you started screaming?"

The horses had finished drinking and turned to the bright green grass upon the bank, but Boon kept his gaze riveted upon hers.

"It was too late. We were out in the middle of nowhere and the sun was setting. I realized that soon I would be alone in the dark with a man I did not know. I asked him if my father's partner, Robbie Cox, would be there."

"Your father's partner is Sam Coats."

Laurie smiled. "Yes. Robbie Cox was, and still is, the man who sells eggs to my mother in Fort Worth. Katz told me that Mr. Cox would be there."

"Clever."

"If I were then I certainly would not have gotten in that wagon in the first place. I thought to run but then realized that there was little in the way of cover and as you rightly pointed out my pastel overskirts and white lace trim seemed to glow in the dark while Katz's clothing blended perfectly with his surroundings. There was a rifle on the floorboards between us. I dropped my reticule. Katz glanced at it but then returned his attention to the team. I made a grab for the rifle, but the barrel hit the seat on the way up, and Katz backhanded me." She pointed at the welt on her left cheekbone. "The same place Hammer hit me."

The muscle in Boon's jaw bulged and his eyes went cold.

"He used the rifle butt to hit me here." She pointed at her midsection. "I lost my wind, but I got one good kick in and retrieved the rifle, but riders appeared firing at close range. I thought for a moment that they were my father's men. But it was George Hammer. He told me to drop it. I didn't at first. I remember thinking that if I lifted the barrel he'd shoot me and I wondered if that was my best choice. But I did as he ordered. The next thing he did was shoot Katz in the head. Then he hog-tied me and tossed me in the back of the buckboard. I was only in camp a few hours before you turned up. Long hours. Hard hours. I knew what they were planning and I kept regretting dropping that gun."

"You a good shot?" he asked.

She didn't mean to brag but she was as good as any cowpoke. "Not as good as my father's men."

He reached into his saddle bags, rummaged for a moment and withdrew a bit of oiled muslin wrapped about something that looked suspiciously like a gun. He unfolded the cloth and revealed a pistol.

"Derringer," she said, accepting the weapon

he handed to her butt-first. Laurie ran her fingers over the well-oiled barrel, taking in the nicks and scars.

He smiled. "Double-shot pocket model. Loaded. It was my mother's."

Chapter Six

Her gaze flashed to his but he said nothing more. A lady didn't pry, but oh, how she wanted to ask. Somehow she held her tongue.

"You know how to switch from one barrel to the next?"

She nodded, gripping the weapon's worn handle. It was an older model, the kind of weapon a gentleman concealed in a vest pocket or a lady in a reticule. She cracked open the breach to find the weapon loaded. Her gaze flashed to Boon. She could shoot him if she chose to. His eyes told her he knew it. Giving her a loaded weapon proved everything he told her was true or he was the craziest man she'd ever met.

"You keep it," he said.

She nodded, her mouth still gaping as she blinked at him. He smiled.

"Might have that same choice again or maybe you can take someone with you."

He hadn't given her a gun. He'd given her a chance and the power to choose. She stared up at him, the gratitude welling in her throat. Laurie felt the urge to tell him why she'd really put away her britches. But she couldn't trust him with that. It would change how he thought of her. Change everything between them. She clutched the derringer to her chest.

"Thank you. I was so afraid they'd ruin me, that my father would be too late and he wouldn't want me back and that no decent man would ever want me."

His scowl grew deeper and the corners of his mouth turned down.

Laurie continued. "Once a woman has been through something like this…well, she'd not be welcomed home. If they find out what has become of me, I fear they may still think the worst. No man wants a woman who's been cruelly used."

"There's men out there who aren't so hard."

"None that I know. That's why a lady must protect her reputation at all costs. I had hopes of attracting a good, decent man. One who is respected in the community. A minster, perhaps, or a banker. A man who I could be proud to call my own."

Boon scrubbed his hand over his mouth, but it didn't remove the bitter taste there. Something curled up and died inside him at her words. He wasn't sure why he should care what kind of a man she wanted to hook. But he did.

"A woman's reputation and that of her family is all she has," Laurie explained.

"I'll tell your father I reached you in time."

She lowered her chin and glanced away. She knew that was not true. A proper lady would have stopped him last night. A proper lady would not have enjoyed his caresses. A proper lady would not be wanting him to touch her again. She couldn't understand her own mind. He was dangerous and not at all the sort of man of which her family would approve, yet there was something to him. He'd brought her clothes, he'd released her bonds, accepted her riding without a lead line and now he'd given her his mother's derringer. That made him an unusual kind of outlaw at the very least.

"What about what happened between us?" she whispered.

"That don't change nothing, Laurie."

Laurie felt the shock clear down to her toes. He'd touched her in the most intimate way possible and it had changed her because she'd enjoyed it. And now she wasn't searching for ways to prevent him from touching her. Quite the opposite. But he said it didn't change a thing? She tore her gaze away but his voice followed her.

"Unless you think the opinion of an outlaw is as valueless as Confederate currency."

She stiffened and then returned her attention to him, finding the hard lines about his mouth had returned. "I said no such thing."

He tugged at the brim of his hat, drawing it low on his forehead. "Your eyes did."

Laurie's chin began to tremble as she looked up at Boon.

"What if my family doesn't want me back?"

Boon could not stand to see her tears. He gathered her in his arms and she relaxed against him, letting him have part of her weight. He rocked her and she let him hold her, let him stroke the satin of her dark hair.

"What if they find out what we did together?" she whispered.

He stiffened and then let the wind leave him with his hope. "What I did *to* you, you mean."

Her big dark eyes widened and she shook her head.

"I didn't stop you."

"Why should you? I only thought to give you ease. Distract you. Comfort you."

She had her hands up over her eyes again as if she couldn't bear to look at him. It muffled her words, but he could make them out.

"I never should have let you."

"Laurie, I swear, I never knew that you'd feel so low about it. You're inexperienced or you'd know that you're still a…well, you're as I found you."

Rather than reassure, this information seemed to be the push that sent her into sobs. Why, try as he might, could he do nothing right by her?

She was gasping for air now and he was rubbing her back, trying to help her along. Why the devil had he believed anything that Paulette had told him? He closed his eyes and recalled how furious the others were when they discovered the tricks she'd taught him.

Paulette had shown him all the ways to please a woman, for her sake, not his. When Lottie and Patsy found out they'd run her out. The two whores at the Blue Belle, where he'd been born, had done their best to raise him after his mother's passing and thought he was too young to be bedded by Paulette, though they'd had customers of the same age and younger. He'd run off after Paulette, thinking himself in love.

When he caught her, she'd set him straight and cut him loose. He'd never confused love and lust again. One was common, the other rare as gold ore.

"I guess I don't know any better," he said. "I never been around ladies before and I didn't figure—"

She drew back so fast he wobbled. "Are you mocking me?"

"Mocking? Laurie, I don't understand."

"You don't think I'm a lady, do you? And why should you? I certainly have not behaved like one."

She sniffed and placed a fist over her mouth. The sight of her in such a state punched a hole through his heart.

"I think you're pretty as a picture, Laurie, and you're a lady if I ever seen one."

She gave a little cry and turned her back, leaving him standing there wanting to hit something, to hold her and also wishing he could roll back time and try again. He was a damned fool.

"My father won't want me back. Not when they know what's happened to me."

"He'll want you back, Laurie. I know it."

"How could you possibly?" she asked, spinning to face him once more as she scrutinized his face.

He couldn't tell her that he knew it because her father had been willing to send the likes of him. He hesitated. Her eyes narrowed on him.

Boon rubbed his neck. "I heard him say so."

The suspicion did not lift from her expression. "What did my father say exactly?"

"Let me think on it a minute."

Boon recalled the summons he'd received to go to the captain's office. He had pushed down the flash of panic that ripped into his insides like lightning through dead wood and made his way across the dusty street to the Cactus Flower Hotel in San Antonio. After his capture and release, Boon had done nothing to make the captain regret his decision not to hang him. But his men had made it clear they wanted justice.

Boon wanted something else. He wanted John Bender's respect. He wanted it so badly he was near cross-eyed with it. John Bender was a legend with the Texas Rangers and

Boon knew what the man had risked by letting him walk.

As he had approached the upstairs room past flickering oil lamps, the raised voices had brought him to a stop.

"I don't care. I want her back." That was Captain Bender's voice, he knew.

"Hammer knows that. He's going to take it out on her. Make her pay for what you did to his brother. He won't get to her in time. You know that." This voice belonged to Sam Coats, Captain Bender's second in command and a Ranger who hated Boon on sight. That's when Coats had said that reforming outlaws was akin to reforming rattlesnakes: the chances of success were not worth the risk.

"I'm not leaving her with Hammer."

They were talking about the soulless outlaw who'd captured him. But who was the *her?* Boon's body tensed as he leaned closer to the door.

"He's only been with them a week. He's not one of them. They'll likely shoot him on sight. It's a mistake."

Boon's heart pounded because he'd ridden with Hammer one week.

"Well, it's *my* mistake."

That was the captain's voice, deep and

commanding. He was a hard man to sway in discussion, though it didn't stop Coats from trying.

Boon's heart now beat in his throat as Coats's words confirmed that he was the subject of their heated discussion.

"I don't trust a man with but one name."

"Not everyone has a family tree stretching back to Jamestown," said the captain, not trying to disguise the irritation in his voice. "Besides, he's the only one with a chance to get in."

"We can take them. You don't need an inside man," said Coats.

"I do if I want her alive."

"Then send Dewey. They don't know him."

"They'd shoot him before he even got off his horse. I need someone who knows how they think. Understands what it takes to ride with them and is willing to do what's necessary to achieve his mission."

"Break the law and murder folks, you mean."

Boon held his breath, waiting, hoping that the captain would defend him. But instead, he said nothing to this.

"You'll get Laurie killed," said Coats.

"He's the fastest rider I've got. Shit, if

Dewey hadn't shot his horse we'd never have caught him."

"Maybe you should send his horse."

"They'd never expect it, for me to send someone like Boon."

What did he mean, someone like him? Someone like an outlaw, a killer? His head sunk. Why had he thought he had a shot at earning the captain's respect? He would always be a rattlesnake, dangerous and unpredictable.

Coats's voice came again, low like a warning whispered in the dark. "He'll turn on you."

Inside the room a chair scraped on the wooden planking.

"Maybe—maybe not. Let's see which way he swings before we give him that rope necktie," said the captain. "I see something in the boy. Give him a chance."

Coats made a sound of frustration. "They say if you give a man enough rope he'll hang himself. If only."

"Where is the boy?"

Boon grimaced. He was no boy. He'd be nineteen come winter. That's what he had been told, anyway. Winter 1862, though none could recall the month or day.

And in the time he'd been with Hammer's

gang he went places and did things that aged him beyond his eighteen years, things that he feared would take a lifetime to forget. Did the captain think him worthy of redemption or was he just waiting for confirmation that he was just as bad as the men he rode with?

"Probably out stealing our horses," said Coats.

He retreated and then made a second approach without his customary stealth. Hammer once said he was the only man he knew who could catch a mountain lion sleeping.

Boon's boots slapped the planking with the confident tread he'd never had. He knocked on the door and waited for the order to enter.

Inside, he found Coats seated in one of two stuffed chairs, his familiar glare now fixed on Boon. Beside him stood Bender, tall and thin, in his black trousers and silver belt buckle, brown leather vest with concho buttons and a clean white shirt. Hard riding and outdoor living made his face tanned and craggy. His long nose was punctuated by a bristly mustache, still black, though the hair on his head showed silver at the temples and at the long sideburns that didn't quite reach his mustache. His gun and holster sat coiled on the table before him.

Coats noticed the direction of Boon's gaze

and made a point of resting a hand on his repeater. Seemed Coats still thought he was here to kill them. As if getting caught was all some master plan to infiltrate the Rangers. They'd shot his horse and taken his weapons, all but the derringer he kept in the inside vest pocket. They'd never looked there. Besides he'd had opportunity to shoot them when they pinned him. He didn't, though he'd expected them to shoot him.

But how could anyone who came from a band of outlaws ever anticipate that once captured, instead of a prompt hanging, he would find mercy?

Boon rubbed his neck. He still didn't understand it. But it did earn his allegiance to the captain. No one ever cared about him before. And no one ever thought he merited a second chance. He would walk through fire for Bender and he'd stay to be insulted by his men because of their captain. Respect wasn't given easily by Rangers.

"You sent for me, Captain?"

"Yes, son. Sit down."

Son; he said it so easily. Did he know that Boon would give his shooting hand to really be this man's son? He lowered his gaze to the floor, not wanting him to see the emotion caused by that simple word. For a man who didn't even know his father's name, the fantasy held great allure.

He sat on the edge of the bed, leaving the good chair for Bender, who folded his lanky frame into the seat beside Coats.

"I've got an assignment for you, son."

Boon's fingers clutched at the rough wool blanket upon the bed as he met the captain's steady gaze. Boon had waited weeks for this, a chance to prove his worth, show he could be one of them, instead of grooming horses and running errands. But this was not what he had pictured, not at all.

"Yes, sir."

"It's dangerous."

Boon nodded, hope surging. The more dangerous the assignment, the better the chance of earning this man's esteem and perhaps, someday, his own peso star. The Texas Rangers wore the star on their coat or hat and it was famously cut from a Mexican silver peso. Boon wanted one of his own. But this was not a prize he could steal. Perhaps he'd never be worthy, but it didn't stop him from dreaming of being a part of this elite group of lawmen.

"Yes, sir?"

"It involves your former associates."

The knot returned to his stomach. It was just as he'd feared. They were sending him back to Hammer.

Boon stared at Bender. Here were two men equally as tough, hardened like the steel barrels of their pistols, but somehow they'd kept their humanity. They held the violence in check and lacked the mercilessness for which Hammer was known.

"I need you to go back to him."

Boon felt he might be sick right there on the captain's bed.

Coats lifted a hand in his direction and smiled. "Look at him. He ain't got the stomach for it."

Boon forced himself to lift his chin and hold the dismissive glare of Sam Coats. "Maybe I'm not good enough for the Rangers. But I'm sure as hell not as bad as that outlaw."

"I know it," said Bender. "And I'm not asking you to join them again, son. He's captured a girl. I need to get her back."

Boon swallowed. Likely her family wouldn't want her once Hammer and his men finished with her. It was the worst part of riding with them, seeing what they did to the women. But the captain had said *girl*.

"You're the only one who can get close

enough to find out where they are. Go back to him. Convince him you're joining up again and then send word to me where you are. Then protect that gal with your life until we get there. Her name's Laurie. Dark hair, dark eyes, pretty as a picture. They took her right here in San Antonio, right under my damned nose, then left a ransom note."

"I know where they might have taken her."

He gave the location of Hammer's two hide-outs and the men decided that the one west of town was the most likely. But when he'd found it deserted he'd sent word back to Bender with a new rendezvous outside of Fort Concho.

"So you'll do it?" asked Bender.

Boon nodded, accepting the assignment. They were sending him back to the thieves and murderers. They'd saved him from hanging but now he'd have to do things that turned his stomach.

"Yes, sir."

"Let me be clear. I want you to take any action necessary to keep that girl alive. I want her back no matter what her condition."

No matter what her condition. That was what Captain John Bender had told him on that last night before he'd headed out to find

Bender's daughter. Only he hadn't told him that Laurie was his child.

The memory of the conversation was fresh as if the captain stood right beside them. All the worry roiled within Boon. How far back was Hammer now?

Boon looked into the dark eyes of Laurie Bender and repeated her father's words verbatim. Laurie gasped when he said "no matter what her condition." Boon didn't repeat that the captain had also told Boon that if he tried to run he'd hunt him down. The captain did not make idle threats.

"I told him where Hammer's camps are. He and his men are nearby. We just got to get out of this here canyon."

He glanced over the horses' backs at the trail they had traveled, a path cut by mule deer. How he prayed it didn't end against a cliff face. He needed to get Laurie home, for he surely did not know how to care for her. The best he could do now was to see her safe and leave her behind.

Boon returned his attention to her face and was cut to ribbons by her sad dark eyes and bruised, swollen cheek.

"They're still back there, Laurie, and our horses aren't spent."

She studied him a moment. “You don’t think we’ll make it, do you?”

Boon sighed. “He’s got more horses.”

Laurie thrust the pistol into the back pocket of her britches, retrieved the reins of her mount.

“But I’ve got you.”

He thought that was poor consolation, but said nothing as he collected the reins of the horses, now busy snatching hanks of the grass that grew beside the river, staining the bits green with their chewing.

“Your father will meet us at the stage station outside of Fort Concho.”

“Why didn’t he come himself?”

Should he tell her? He looked into her dark, earnest eyes. They were nearly the same age, he figured, yet he felt decades older.

“Mr. Boon, please do tell me the truth. I have been sheltered, but I am not faint of heart.”

He nodded, his decision made. Laurie had already proved her mettle last night in the camp and during the long ride. He’d never met a woman who could sit a horse like she had, in the dark, up and down rough trails. “First sign of pursuit, Hammer kills all prisoners and their horses. Your pa knew he couldn’t fetch you alive. I'm sorry he had to send someone like me, Laurie. But he did the best he could. 'Spect that the Rangers wouldn't have done to you what I did. 'Spect they know how to act around a lady. Guess that's why I ended up like I have." He stared at her. Damn, he'd turn a cartwheel if he thought it would cheer her. "We'll ride along this stream until we get out of this box. Figure the horses might last another few hours."

She didn't ask what they would do when the horses were spent. A few hours wouldn't be enough time to reach the station, but he wouldn't dare tell her that.

Laurie allowed Boon to help her up, though they both knew she didn't need it. He was glad for the excuse to touch her again and angry at himself for wanting her so much. Then he vaulted into the saddle and they were off again. The stream grew wider. Dry season was approaching and most streambeds never saw water except for the spring and summer. They were lucky to reach a draw that showed life. But would their luck hold?

Chapter Seven

Laurie was so tired she could barely keep her eyes open. Her back now throbbed and needles of pain were punctuated with occasional stabs. The horses' heads hung and their hides glistened with sweat. Still Boon rode on. If they rode their mounts to death, how would they escape Hammer?

She clamped her teeth together to keep from begging him to stop. When his horse began to stagger, he finally pulled up.

Laurie glanced at the sky to see the sun was well into its descent. She figured that they had been riding nearly twenty hours. As the horses stopped, Laurie lifted her head and glanced around them. They had been climbing but now she saw they were no longer in a narrow canyon surrounded with high walls, but a wide V between two rocky hills. Boon had found a way out of the draw.

Boon dismounted and headed back for her, with a strong, even stride that showed no evidence of the bone-weakening fatigue that now gripped her.

He assisted her down, holding her only as long as it took for her to recover her equilibrium before stepping back. Was it regret or consternation she saw in his eyes?

"I'll see to the horses," he said. "They'll need to graze some and rest. But we'll ride on after dark."

Laurie swayed on rubbery legs and staggered. Boon caught her elbow.

"What's wrong?"

"My legs are numb." It was her bottom that was numb but she couldn't very well say that. Mention of her legs was bad enough, but there they were, sheathed in trousers for all to see. She also discovered, to her horror, that her bladder was fairly bursting.

Boon saw her safely back on her feet and then gave her a critical stare.

"I just need a moment."

He nodded, not looking convinced at all, but turned to his chestnut gelding, releasing the cinch and throwing the girth across the seat before dragging off the saddle and blanket in one unit. His horse gave an audible sigh of relief. Boon checked the horses' backs for sores as Laurie headed toward the cottonwoods for some privacy. As they had journeyed upstream, the undergrowth had become so thick that they had to follow an animal path, just beyond the trees. She had seen only flashes of water since then.

"Where you going?" Boon's voice halted her.

She paused, but did not look back. "I just need some privacy."

The response met with silence. She turned to find him holding the second saddle and blanket, his eyes pinned on her.

"Don't go far."

She nodded and made a hasty escape.

His voice trailed her. "And watch for snakes."

Laurie froze, her bladder forgotten amid the possibility of seeing that most hated of creatures. Her flesh crawled as she began a careful search of the ground about her. Finally the urging of her body set her in motion. Once in cover she checked the ground and poked about with a stick before wrestling with the rivets and stiff denim. The breeze was warm on her privates as she squatted in the grass and quickly saw to business. *I need to get my clothing back,* she decided. Her outer lavender traveling attire was not designed for riding, but the dark underskirts beneath were ample and would not reveal them in the moonlight. She lifted Boon's fawn-colored neckerchief and stared down at her constricted bosom. *Well, no wonder he was aroused by you. You look like a pink lady.*

Her own clothes, she decided, would help remove temptation from him. If she dressed as a lady, he would treat her like one. Or she hoped so. Did it take a wicked man to recognize a wicked woman?

She stood and forced the rivets closed. When she retraced her steps, she discovered the horses hobbled and Boon standing in the place she had left his sight.

"Did you drink?" he asked.

She hadn't, though she was thirstier than she had ever been in her life. That likely accounted for why she could hold her water so long.

"I didn't know if it was safe."

"I hear running water. Let's go see."

She didn't move. "I want my clothes back."

He frowned. “These are more practical.”

“If I were a boy, they would be. But we both saw last night how impractical they are.”

He couldn’t meet her gaze and looked quickly away then back, a definite defensive glitter in his eyes.

She motioned with her hand. “My clothing, please.”

He gave her an exasperated look. “Easy to spot you in that.”

“My skirts.”

He spun to the saddles and bags, dragging out the wrinkled lavender damask outer skirts and solid violet underskirt. She saw, as he held it aloft, that the underskirt was torn at the knee and stained with red mud all about the hem.

Boon returned with the rumpled garment and handed it off to her. The snowy blouse was secreted in the skirts, but both the detachable front ruffle and the damask basque bodice were missing. She waited. He offered nothing more.

“What about my bodice?”

He pressed his lips tighter.

“My underthings?” Her voice changed of its own accord, transitioning from the stern tone she intended and dissolving into desperation.

His face flushed and his eyes narrowed. This was how he looked when he faced Larson.

Laurie took a step back.

"They didn't fit in my bags so I left them."

"You…what?" Laurie sputtered. She was about to tell him that the hoops for the half crinoline and the bustle had been quite dear, costing her almost all of the money she had earned making women's clothing. Her mother had been furious when she discovered Laurie had been taking in piecework for pay. The fact that Laurie had colluded with Paloma, using their housekeeper as a front, did little to douse her mother's fiery temper. Her mother wanted her daughter to have the skills to run a household but that did not include working like a common seamstress. Needlepoint and tatting were one thing, dressmaking quite another. When her mother found out that Laurie had learned sewing at the finishing school, she had taken it up with the headmistress and removed her from her charge.

Her mother had adequate funds to support them, but not for fashions she deemed inappropriate. Laurie's father still sent money for Laurie's care, according to what Paloma had told her, but her mother was stubborn and would not touch it, except to deposit it into the bank.

Paloma said she didn't need his money, which was true because her mother had an inheritance bequeathed from her grandparents and expected Laurie to learn from her mistake and keep clear of lawmen and cowboys. *Her* daughter would marry a man who could afford to provide her with servants.

But Laurie had coveted the fashions she'd seen in the magazines and she'd found a way to get what she wanted without her mother. Now Boon had tossed away her most prized outfit.

"You had absolutely no right to do that!"

Boon set his jaw and stared her down. "Thought the water and ammunition was more important than ruffles and gewgaws."

She gasped, making indignant noises in her throat. He was right, of course, and that only served to annoy her further. Laurie snatched what remained of her garments from him, unsure what to do next. Boon provided the answer.

"We gotta stay here, close to the trees, until the horses are rested."

"How long?"

"Hour, maybe two. Time enough to eat, refill the canteen and wash if you've a mind to."

Suddenly, washing away the dirt and sand

from her body seemed more important than food or rest.

"Yes, a bath," she said.

His eyebrows tented. "Bath? Well, I reckon that'd be all right."

He led the way, taking a small path through the wooded area and past the heavy undergrowth. As they approached, she could hear the rush and tumble of moving water, but it was not until they cleared the thorny underbrush and broke from the tall grass that she saw the cascading waterfall, some eight feet high. They stared up at the water rushing in rivulets down three tiers of one massive stone outcropping worn smooth by the water's flow. It was obvious by the size of the gap that the water thundered down this incline at times, but now seemed gentle and welcoming as summer rain.

"Oh, it's lovely."

Boon studied their surroundings, his judgment less aesthetic.

"Clean water and not too deep. Let me just clear it for snakes and you can have your bath."

The word *snakes* put a damper on her enthusiasm and she contented herself with following him through the tall grass, eyes pinned on the ground. He glanced back at her.

"They're in the trees, too," he said as casually as one might comment on the weather.

Laurie now walked in his footsteps, huddling against him as if expecting to be attacked from all sides.

"You don't like snakes?" he asked.

"Of course I don't like snakes. Who in the world does like them?"

He shrugged. "Serve a purpose. They remove the vermin. Deadly, persistent, and they get the job done, like Texas Rangers."

"I rather think there are significant differences between the two."

He shrugged again and continued walking until they stood upon the flat rock that gradually inclined beneath the water. Beyond, the cottonwood and oak trees climbed up the hillside adjoining the falls.

She looked longingly at the water. "Can we afford to stop? The outlaws might catch us."

"They might. But we can't get away on spent horses. You wash up. Swim if you know how."

"I know how."

She gave her a speculative look. "Shooting and riding and swimming. Not your typical gal, are you, Laurie?"

"When I was young, my father taught me

those things, before my mother took me in hand."

"Those things, as you call them, kept you on that horse last night in rough territory. Uncommon to teach a woman something so necessary." He motioned toward the water. "Go on. Call if you need me."

She cast him an incredulous look. "You'll not spy on me?"

He tugged his hat low on his brow and his eyes turned cold. "Laurie, I may be just an outlaw, but I keep my word. I'll see to the horses." With that he left her standing beside the inviting water.

She waited, glancing back toward the brush, into which he had vanished. When she was certain he had gone she felt suddenly afraid and nearly called him back, but she looked out at the water, which reflected the lovely leafy greenery surrounding her, and succumbed to the desire to immerse herself in the secluded pool beneath the gentle falls.

Her gloves went first and she checked her hands for freckles. Finding none, she sat to unlace her boots, removing them and then her stockings. She glanced back again and found Boon nowhere in sight. She had to peel out of her denim dungarees, feeling a bit like an onion losing its outer skin. She worked the buttons from the roughly sewn buttonholes on the boys' shirt with impatience and drew off the garment, finally feeling the breeze caress her bare shoulders. The corset gave her trouble as the knots held fast. She exhaled to gain enough play to wiggle the tether free and then released the cording, drawing the first full breath she had managed since dressing yesterday morning.

She stood on the bank in her knee-length chemise feeling suddenly free. She tipped her head back to the wide blue sky and stretched. She had not bathed out of doors since she was a girl. She drew the tan-colored kerchief, which Boon had lent her, over her head and sat upon the warm flat rock. Laurie worked her fingers through her hair and carefully collected the tenacious pins that still clung along with the single comb. She took a moment to mourn the loss of its mate, a lovely turtle shell that had been a gift last year from her mother on her seventeenth birthday. Laurie scratched her scalp in a most unladylike fashion and shook out her hair. Standing, she tugged her chemise over her head and tossed it aside.

Unbound and unfettered, she waded into the pool, which was only cool enough to be refreshing. The water lapped about her hips. The stream bottom seemed to be one rocky shelf that was not so steep as to be slippery. She found the pool only as deep as her rib cage, but she sank gratefully into the water and crept toward the waterfall, using it to drench her head and cool her. She closed her eyes and let the water pour over her, washing away the dust and grime and fear. No bath in her entire life had ever been more welcome.

She scrubbed and splashed and paddled and even dunked a time or two. Laurie was a good swimmer thanks to her father's lessons. It was in the midst of this frolic that she had the unsettling feeling that someone was watching her. She stilled, wiped the water from her eyes and then glanced around. Nothing moved on the bank or in the water. Had Hammer found them?

She turned in a slow circle and saw the tuft of grass on the far bank moving. Something was coming. A moment later a huge rattlesnake as big around as her wrist splashed into the water undulating right at her. A scream tore from her as she spun, half running, half swimming in the opposite direction.

"Boon! Help!"

Chapter Eight

The snake pursued Laurie as she dashed toward the bank, heading for the derringer she'd left with her skirts. The snake slithered closer, its brown-and-black body undulating in a sinuous contortion.

Any moment that rattler would sink its venomous fangs into her. Laurie's heart pounded as she raced away.

Boon darted down the rock, scrambling on all fours, pistol in one hand, his body naked and honed. The sight of him just as bare as she was stopped her momentarily as she stared in stunned silence, taking in the sheer beauty of all that moving muscle.

Recalling her peril, Laurie pointed.

"Rattlesnake!" she screeched.

His eye tracked the snake, but instead of shooting, he jumped into the water behind her to intercept. The snake moved to avoid, but Boon snatched it up, capturing the reptile just behind the head.

Was he insane? The snake writhed, coiling about his bare forearm. Laurie gaped at Boon, thinking she would never forget the sight of him, naked, water streaming down his chest as he gripped the snake in his left hand and his pistol in the right. He looked from the snake to her, grinning with pride as if he were seven and had just captured a newt instead of a deadly serpent.

She meant to order him to put it down, wondering why he didn't have more sense. But her body was now going haywire, not from the snake, but from seeing his abdomen flex and the large muscles of his chest cord, as he brought the snake closer to his face. Her voice had abandoned her.

She glanced down to his male member swinging just above the water's surface and felt a thrill of excitement steal her breath. She met his gaze and watched the pride at his capture turn to realization that they were both standing naked in knee-deep water.

Laurie gave a cry of alarm and then clamped

her hands over her eyes. A moment later she realized this did nothing to shield her nudity from him.

She was half furious and half mortified that he had discovered her like this. Why had she removed her chemise or not just washed herself quickly beneath her skirts while she still wore them? Any reasonable woman would have done just that, of course. But not her! No, she had stripped down to her nothing-at-all and gone swimming before God and everyone.

Laurie made a dash for the shore, tunneling into her chemise and tearing into her underskirt before thrusting her arms into her blouse. She had it mostly on when she glanced back to the pool to find Boon had moved to deeper water, effectively covering what he could without dunking his pistol or the writhing reptile.

"Do you eat snake?" he asked.

"Nooo!" she howled, covering her eyes again.

"For a gal who can ride and shoot and swim, you sure are scared of a little snake."

"Little?" she asked, hands still plastered over her eyes.

"I seen bigger."

"I don't care. I *hate* snakes. Always hated

them. They're sneaky and squirmy and horrible."

"They're not." His voice sounded closer.

She turned her back. There was a splash and then nothing. She peeked between her fingers.

The snake was gone.

She dropped her hands from her face, searching the water as she inched back.

"Where is it?" she asked.

"Swimming downstream, I'd imagine." He gazed at her from the water and she knew she should turn her back. But she didn't.

The water made his blond hair dark and curly at his neck. She wanted to touch all that bronze skin and tempting muscle. That recognition made her turn sideways so that she now stared downstream.

"You've never even tried snake, have you?" His tone held accusation.

Her stomach flipped at the thought of consuming something so vile.

"They're slimy," she said, by way of explanation.

He snorted. "Dry as dirt. The skin, I mean. The meat's real tasty." He was glancing over his shoulder with a look of longing. "Real good."

"Why didn't it rattle?"

"Suppose because it's a water snake," he said.

"What?" She was staring at him again, finding his eyes dancing and his expression now full of mirth. The change in his features transformed him into someone fun-loving and playful. It was like seeing a different person. Laurie's jaw went slack as she stared, captivated.

He pointed downstream. "No rattle on a water snake."

"Poisonous?"

"Nope. Looks more like a water moccasin than a rattler. Hard to confuse a water snake for a rattler. Surprised your pa never taught you about snakes."

"He tried." She shuddered.

Boon laughed. "Some folks are that way about heights. Known a fella who couldn't stand being boxed in. Slept outside every night, even in the rain." His gaze dipped and she realized her wet chemise now clung to her torso like a second skin.

Laurie folded her hands over her chest. "I'm sorry."

He waved a hand at his privates. "Me, too. I was washing downstream when your scream sent me running." His gaze continued to the opposite bank as something occurred to him. "What scared the snake into the water?"

"What?"

"The snake. They don't generally go swimming."

Laurie felt a prickle on her neck as she recalled the grass moving an instant before the snake hit the water.

"Something in that patch of grass." She pointed.

Boon aimed his gun at the opposite bank and waded through the shallow water, exiting at the far side. She blinked in surprise as she noted that his backside was squareish instead of round like her own. She cocked her head, more intrigued than ever as he vanished into the tall grass.

"Coyote," he called. "Big one."

He reappeared and headed toward her. She gobbled up the sight of Boon naked and in motion then recalled herself and spun around, facing the opposite direction. But the image of him scorched into her mind. Laurie made no attempt to erase the picture he made. It was a memory to keep a woman warm on a long winter night. But that was all it could be, said the voice in her head. She stiffened her spine as the splashing grew nearer.

What would he do when he reached her? Laurie braced and then realized she half hoped he would gather her in his arms. Whatever was wrong with her? But she knew. She wasn't afraid of him. She knew he was dangerous but also knew he wasn't dangerous to her. He'd never hurt her, not intentionally at least.

She'd finally set aside her fear of being touched and the man who had done that was an outlaw sent by her father to bring her home safe. Laurie trembled at his approach.

His voice came from close by. "I'll just go get my gear."

She nodded, head bowed demurely. The skin on her scalp began to tingle and she had to squeeze her hand into a fist so she could think. Laurie forced her gaze to remain on the ground.

"I'll wait here."

She heard his wet feet contacting the wide stone bank.

"Be right back," he said.

Laurie didn't keep her eyes averted for long. Despite the strong talking-to she gave herself, she peeked again. The long muscles of his back corded as he swung his arms in an easy stride. With his disappearance, Laurie still felt restless and jumpy.

Did he recognize that she found his naked body as fascinating as he found hers? Of course not, because ladies did not behave that way and she was the daughter of Valencia Sanchez Garcia, a well-born Castilian lady whose family was none too pleased that she had fallen for a wild Texan. Being Castilian, she did not adopt her husband's name upon marrying and continued to be known by her given name, Valencia Sanchez Garcia, to her husband's dismay. It was because of this custom that Laurie's name was recorded as Laurie Garcia Bender.

Laurie's mother was everything Laurie had failed to become: reserved, calm, dignified and proper—or *had* been until she decided to marry a Texan and then divorce him. Laurie felt in her bones that even on her best day she'd never measure up.

Well, she wasn't her mother. Never was and never would be. Laurie looked at the two piles of clothing. The first, the boys' Levis and shirt Boon had provided, and the other, the rumpled remains of the fashionable day dress she had created to prove to the world that she was a lady.

Laurie lifted the corset and threw it with

all her might. The bulky, ungainly thing flew poorly and then fell like a stone into the pool.

She glared at it for a long moment, her fury boiling inside her. She was not that lady, but neither was she the wild child she had once been.

Laurie didn't really know who she was. She only knew that she was not riding in that corset ever again.

"You all right, Laurie?" Boon called.

She didn't think she'd ever be all right again.

Boon waited until Laurie gave the all clear. Then he made his way back to her. He came to an abrupt stop at the sight that greeted him. This woman did not look like Laurie. He took in the changes.

She now stood in only the gauzy blouse and the simpler dark purple pleated skirt. The blouse had been buttoned up tight and the long purple skirt securely fastened about her tiny waist. She held the Levis and boys' shirt in a neatly folded pile before her.

Her wet hair tumbled free about her shoulders, soaking the back of her white blouse, making it transparent so he could see the pink ribbon of her chemise between the gaps left by her dripping curls. He lifted an eyebrow as he noted she did not wear her "armor," as he liked to think of corsets.

Where was it? The answer came when he looked to the pool and saw it lying at the bottom like a drowning victim. A lavender mass of heavy fabric undulated in the moving water, seeming to crawl along the bottom. So she'd abandoned the heavy top skirt, as well, he realized. He cocked his head to study the sodden garment that had once hugged her curvy hips like a caress as it floated downstream.

"You gonna need that?"

"Definitely not."

"But you going to ride in skirts?" he asked.

"They fit more comfortably than trousers." She extended the clothing he'd given her. "Thank you for these."

He accepted the bundle.

"You look different."

"Less like a lady, you mean?"

"No. That ain't it." He shook his head. "More natural, maybe."

She laced her fingers before her and smiled. "I've never liked corsets." Her tone was conspiratorial.

"Me, neither," he said, glancing at the drowned discarded duds.

She giggled. "You've seen a lot of them I suppose—corsets, I mean?"

The question took him back to that hot, dusty room above the saloon overlooking the street. Evenings he'd watched the cowboys come and go as the women who raised him worked just beyond those closed doors. During the drives he'd slept on that balcony, waking covered with a fine later of dirt.

What would Lottie and Patsy think of him today?

They'd done the best they could, but somehow he still felt they'd be disappointed. God knew he was.

"Boon?"

He refocused his attention on Laurie, all fresh and lovely in the bright morning air. Had Lottie once looked like that, open and earnest and eager?

He needed to get Laurie home safe. Keep her from the kind of tough choices a woman with no friends or family was forced into. So why was he again thinking of riding with her toward Mexico?

Her father wasn't likely to let him run off with Laurie. He knew Bender would come after him with everything he had. That's what Boon would do if Laurie was his. But Boon still thought he could outrun them all. He just needed fresh horses.

Laurie looked up at him with such trust. He didn't deserve it.

"I seen my share of everything. I'm weary with it. You don't get quit of me and you'll see it, too."

"I don't understand."

"Nor should you. I pray to God you never understand. Why I seen so many corsets, so many women."

Why did he care what this woman—no, *lady*—thought of him? Damn if only the horses were sound, they could ride. Instead, he was trapped as she was trapped, here, together, alone.

Boon released a long breath he'd been holding and gazed off at the falls, watching the water tumble, feeling his insides tumble. He might have the courage to tell her if she would not look at him with that open expression.

"I didn't have a regular home, Laurie. My ma died bringing me. I never knew her." He cast Laurie a quick glance and then returned his attention to the cascading water.

"I am so sorry."

He nodded mechanically, feeling hard and brittle as dried clay. She started to reach out to him, but he inched away and her hand fell back to her side.

Boon continued to stare out, but now his jaw was working as if he was trying to grind granite to dust between his molars.

"She was a good-time girl."

Laurie gasped. Did it shock her to hear a man call his mother something so black? He wasn't insulting her, just saying what he knew of her. Not all mothers were saints and not all were willing to raise a child. Some never had the chance. How could he miss so much something that he'd never had?

"They all were. When I was born, she called me Boon, but no one knew her last name and she wouldn't tell them for fear the shame of her condition would reach her family. That's why I got no last name. They called her Goldie, but said that weren't her real name, just the color of her hair. That's all I know of her." Lord, he hadn't talked this much in the sum total of a month. Still he forged on, his mouth dry. "She died and left me to Lottie and Patsy, who raised me up with the help of the cook, Griff. He'd been a buffalo soldier. Lost two fingers and part of an ear fighting the Sioux." He thought of Paulette and flushed at the memories. His education, he realized, had been unique. "A cow town has lots of places for the young bucks to spend their pay. I cleaned up, helped Griff." Saw things no boy should ever see, no girl for that matter. "Anyways, I know nothing of my mother except that she hailed from Ohio and wouldn't give me her name. Her life was hard and it was short."

Laurie stood in uneasy silence. She couldn't even meet his eye but fussed unnecessarily with the pleating of her skirts as he wiped his damp palms on his thighs. Where were her gloves?

Now she acted like the ladies he passed on the street, the ones who looked right through him like glass.

He felt himself disappearing, just like he had when he was a boy, sleeping on that porch above the bar. Laurie knew what he was now and that ought to be enough for her to keep her distance. Kissing him had been just a momentary weakness that had later humiliated her. Women were weak and men were persuasive—wasn't that what Lottie had always said?

Laurie forced herself not to fidget as she stood beneath his perusal, but had to clasp her hands together to manage it. He'd told her something very personal but also very inappropriate for a lady to hear. Part of her wanted to offer comfort, but she also knew she should not broach this subject. She paused, pondering what to do.

"I guess ladies don't talk about whores. From what I seen they just sort of pretend they don't exist, like they're invisible."

Laurie met his troubled gaze and nodded. "Yes. That's right."

"But they ain't. They're just unlucky. When you got no options you fall into all kinds of trouble. I need to get you home before you see any more of how damned hard things are."

Laurie wondered what options she'd have if word got out of what had befallen her, and cringed. Could he see her tremble? Boon stared at her with cold, clear eyes, then turned to the water, dismissing her from his attention. Silence stretched. Laurie watched him and fidgeted, clicking her index fingernail against her thumbnail and only belatedly realized she had lost her gloves. Why wouldn't he look at her?

She could feel him withdrawing back into his shell, rolling up like an armadillo.

"Did they look through you, too, Boon?"

His troubled gaze flicked back to her and she knew it was so. She stepped closer and the pull between them resurfaced, like a rope, strung tight between the two, keeping them from breaking free.

"Oh, hell," he muttered.

"What?"

"I thought you had more sense. I just told you about my people. If that don't send you off, I don't know what will."

Is that why he told her, to make her run? Instead his willingness to share something so intimate and so painful drew her in. He wasn't fearless as he seemed. He wasn't hard and unfeeling like the men who rode with Hammer. And like her, his pain had shaped him.

Did he really think she would ever treat him as if he were beneath her?

"Is that why you told me?"

"Hell, yes. One of us has to show some sense."

What he had done now seemed all the more endearing. He'd revealed a personal part of himself that she knew he never spoke about, and all to help do as he promised and keep her safe, not just from outlaws and snakes but from the attraction that tugged between them even now.

Why couldn't she feel this way for a respectable man? Then she had another thought: why couldn't Boon be respectable?

But that was impossible—wasn't it? Her heart ached as she considered the possibility and then was forced to let the notion go. He might be able to keep her safe out here, but he was rough and raw and her parents would never let such a man near her if not for the dire circumstances.

He glared at her, as if he knew her thoughts, making her feel she was again the unwelcome burden with which he'd been saddled. But she saw through him now. The anger glinting in his eyes was just his defense against the pain. Boon cloaked himself in fury. She could almost see the chip he carried on his shoulders.

Laurie gathered herself to do what she must.

"Thank you for not taking advantage of the situation in which you just found me."

He cocked his head and regarded her for a long silent moment, assessing something. Could he read the truth there on her face—see that his revelation had backfired and now she found him even more appealing? He had secrets, too.

He readjusted his gray hat. "I won't take what you don't offer."

"You don't act like an outlaw."

"Many would disagree."

They walked side by side to the yellowing grass where the horses fed.

"Men are supposed to be tempted, I think," she said.

He glanced at her and then away. "Women, too."

Laurie felt her heartbeat accelerate. He'd know, of course, from his upbringing and his own experiences. Up until her meeting with Boon, she'd never believed it, had secretly wondered how a woman could stand a man's touch and to let him do the things necessary to have children. Now she thought she understood because Boon stirred her desire effortlessly.

"A lady isn't supposed to," she whispered, thinking she'd never really been a lady.

He took hold of her shoulders and gently turned her so she now stared at his chest.

"Laurie, look at me."

She didn't want to, but she did, lifting her gaze as her ears burned hot.

"Women got the same needs as men. Don't you know that?"

She stared up at him. "I didn't. Until I met you."

His hands slipped away and he stepped back. She followed him with her eyes.

"I had a beau in Fort Worth," she said. "His father owned a large hardware store. Charles was very sweet and had good prospects. Mother encouraged me but…"

Her shoulders rose and fell. She fiddled with the nail of her index finger. But she didn't speak.

"But what?"

"When he tried to kiss me, I froze up inside. I didn't like it because…I just didn't." She peeked up at him and then away. "Every time he came near me, I did the same thing. Finally he stopped courting me. Mother was furious but I was…relieved."

"Well, he wasn't the fella for ya. That's all."

Her hands fisted at her sides and her chin took on a stubborn quality. "He was *exactly* the fellow for me. He was handsome, kind, well-off, with prospects. He was just the sort I thought I wanted. So why couldn't I let him hold me, but I let you…" She waved her hand at him.

Boon stiffened as his eyes narrowed at the insult.

"Guess hardware boy didn't know women

like I do. You just need to find a feller knows how to please."

A man like him. She took another step in his direction.

"But maybe you want to find one that don't have a wanted poster attached to his name."

Laurie stopped moving, torn again between what was best and what she wanted.

Chapter Nine

"Laurie, you're scared and you're alone and I'm the best chance you got. But what you're feeling is coming from all that confusion. You just hold tight a little longer and I'll get you home. We follow this stream out of the canyon."

He pointed, drawing her attention away from himself and back to their journey. Reluctantly she followed the direction he indicated.

"From there I've only got to get you to the stage station just shy of Fort Concho. Your pa is meeting us there. We just have to stay ahead of the Hammer for one more night and we're home free."

He escorted her back to the horses where he retrieved two cans and a skillet from his bags.

They returned to the rock beside the stream because Boon thought it a better spot to cook.

"Won't they see the smoke?"

"I'll keep the fire low and close to the rock face. Be real hard to spot. Have to be right on top of us to see the smoke. Besides, safer to have a small fire in daylight than at night."

She helped him gather dead wood for a fire.

She didn't think she was hungry until he punctured the cans with his knife and heated them in the skillet. The aroma made her mouth water and she tried to recall her last meal. Breakfast, before departing on the train, she recalled. Poached eggs, buttered toast and strong tea.

Boon turned his knife to a stick they'd collected for the fire and quickly carved a shallow paddlelike spoon for her as the beans and beef heated. They ate straight from the pan, she with her new spoon and he with the back of his knife now functioning as a sort of shovel. When they finished they sat back against the fallen log to rest a moment.

"Do we have to go now?" she asked.

He glanced at the sky and nodded. "Soon."

She followed his gaze noting the change in the sun's angle before returning her focus to him. "Thank you. That was the best thing I've eaten in days," she said.

He glanced up at her. "The only thing you've eaten in days. I can lay out a pretty nice spread when I have the fixings. I do baking, too."

She lifted her brows at that. Most men could open a can of beans, but did not really know their way about a kitchen.

"Are you teasing me?"

"Nope. I used to make the bread at the Blue Belle."

He was just full of surprises, she thought. Like her, he wasn't at all what he appeared.

He reached for the skillet, now cool and empty, and then paused. He remained still just a moment and then stood, bringing the skillet to the water. But now he was silent.

She knew instantly something was wrong again. Was it his mention of the Blue Belle? Curiosity tugged at her. Laurie wanted to know everything about him, but after the last time, when he'd told her about his mother and then practically ran her off, she went slow.

Laurie followed him to the stream, sitting beside him as he dipped the skillet and scrubbed it with wet sand.

"Who taught you?" She held her breath, expecting him to slam down the skillet or storm away, but he did neither, just continued the rhythmic sweep of sand over the cast iron.

"I used to work in the kitchen with Griff at the house. Brought the girls their meals sometimes." He kept his eyes averted, as if he was too embarrassed by what he said to hold his head up.

It made her angry that he should have to feel so ashamed of his boyhood. It was not his choice, after all.

"It's a pity no one thought to bring you away from there."

"Some had worse. Least I had a bed and food. Griff taught me to ride and rope. Gave me my first gun. It was an old gun, but still. Besides, who'd want a rough, foul-mouthed little kid like me underfoot? Nobody could tell me nothing back then, except Griff. I don't know how I've lasted so long."

She wondered about him. Had his upbringing contributed to his choice to join Hammer's band of outlaws? Boon seemed such a contradiction. He was hard and tough, but he seemed to lack the cruelty necessary for such nasty business. She lifted her fingers to probe at her swollen cheek and the scab that remained as evidence of the blows landed by both Katz and Hammer.

It might have been worse. Hammer had swung without restraint. She shuddered to think what would have become of her if he had landed that blow. He hadn't because of Boon. He was as defensive as a guard dog but there was a certain sweetness to him. He'd tended her a little roughly, but perhaps in the best fashion he knew how. So it pained her to think of the end he could expect if he was caught on the wrong side of the law.

Her inquisitiveness warred with the understanding that she had no right to ask him such personal questions. Her manners abandoned her again, beaten back by her need to know him.

"How did you fall in with George Hammer?"

Boon tore a hank of grass up by the roots and used the clean end to dry the skillet, sweeping the long green stalks around and around. He glanced up at her.

"You sure you want to hear this?"

Did she? Laurie paused to consider. She recalled the way he had ended Lawson's life and felt a chill run up her spine. Then she thought of how he'd snatched her from under their very noses. He was brutal, brave and sometimes thoughtful. She had seen two sides of him. Was he a good man or a bad one? Laurie didn't know, but she yearned to discover everything about him.

She nodded. "I do."

He pressed his lips together and drew a great breath as if resigning himself to her request. He sat beside her, drawing up his knees and letting the skillet dangle from one hand.

Dragonflies darted over the water and Laurie noted that the sun now dropped toward the ridge of rock. It would be evening soon and with the dusk, she'd be riding again.

The cold that gripped her now had little to do with the approaching night and all to do with her worry over what he might reveal next.

"Laurie, I've done things I'm not proud of."

His words made her think on her own past mistakes that could never be set right. She understood exactly what that meant.

She felt a connection between them growing. She knew she could resist his handsome face and his melodic voice. But resisting this common ground she recognized between them was harder. Boon made her feel as if she was not the only person in the world trying to live down her past.

Anton never made her feel anything other than obligation and discomfort. But Boon lit her up like the tail of a comet in the night sky. She came alive under his touch and now she felt a connection to him that went bone deep. She knew that she was suddenly on dangerous ground. If she were wise she'd stop him right here, before the sympathy she fostered for him grew even more unwieldy.

"We all have skeletons in our closets, I suppose," she said. Laurie felt a twinge of guilt. Was she asking to find something to repulse her or because she needed to know him better? The latter, she knew, and felt the uncertainty double, filling her stomach and washing through her lungs. She held her breath, hoping he wouldn't answer, hoping he would.

He removed his hat, setting it beside him on the ground. Then he raked his long fingers through his hair and gave the back of his scalp a rub. She itched to run her fingers through that mass of sun-bleached hair. Instead she curled her hands demurely into her lap.

"I don't think I'm supposed to talk about such a topic before a lady."

"I insist."

He considered her for a long moment, rubbing his knuckles over the stubble on his jaw.

"All right then. But remember you asked." He drew a deep breath and plunged in. "After I left them that raised me, I signed on as a bush cowboy, chasing wild cows out of thick cover and bringing them in for branding. Still got the scars on my legs to prove it. Thorns on some of those bushes were this long." He indicated the distance as far as his thumb and index finger could stretch. "Cat claws, they called them. Must have been wildcats, I guess."

He reached for his hat then stayed his free hand and laid it back on his knee, drumming his fingers. Finally he set the skillet beside his hat.

"I couldn't ride very well then and more than once I roped a cow and ended up on the wrong side of a tree on a half-wild pony. Been gored, stomped on and thrown more times than I care to recall. But I learned to ride and rope and earned enough to buy a good pair of chaps." He indicated the ones he wore, scarred though they were. "Next I bought a pistol, then another. I never went into town on Saturday nights like the rest of the boys."

Laurie nodded. "I'd imagine your boyhood had included one too many Saturday nights."

That arrested him. He stared at her a moment and then nodded. "That's right. I just couldn't do to those women what I'd seen done to the ones who raised me. The boys got no idea. They're just looking for a good time, you know? But it's not good. Not good at all. I seen women, good women, forced into such a life because of one mistake. Then they get stuck and can't get out."

She rubbed one hand absently along her opposite arm. What would he think if he knew how narrowly she had escaped such a fate? That she, too, had made that one mistake? If her parents had discovered her disgrace, of what she had allowed Anton to do to her, would they have cast her out? She had told Anton no, but she hadn't fought him and afterward she'd been too ashamed to tell her parents what they had done. A second mistake, she realized. But she'd been so afraid that they'd make her marry him and she couldn't bear the thought of him doing that to her again.

Boon didn't seem to note her distraction as he went on.

"Some get clear, though. Big Mary saved enough. She wrote us from Kansas City and said she was now Mrs. Mary Smith Mann, widow and owner of a respectable boardinghouse. She just made up a new past including a dead husband."

He laughed at that. The musical sound made Laurie's stomach flutter. She inched closer, watching his eyes dance at the memory and watched the humor die a quick death.

"But most, they are too ashamed even to let their kin know what became of them.

"That's why I got no name. My ma would never say it for fear her family might discover how far she'd fallen.

"Anyways, I swore I'd never do that to a woman, never use her body and then just take off. It's not right what men do. I'll never take a woman unless I married her first."

Laurie could not stifle her shock. Never? She struggled with the recognition that in this area, she had more experience than he. The experience had been all bad, but still. Laurie watched Boon as he used a stick to poke a small stone into the water and then tossed the stick in after it. She thought back to what he had done to her that first night. Tried to compare the sweetness, the wildness and the pleasure to the humiliation she had experienced with Anton. Her face grew hot.

"Anyway, this isn't proper talk, I reckon."

She inched back from him and forced a smile. "No. Please go on."

He rubbed the back of his neck and finally stared at her.

"I got into a lot of fights growing up. Tried working in town, but got fired a few times. Never drew my pistols on a man, but I was quick to raise my fists. It felt good to hit someone. I even liked getting hit back."

"But that makes no sense."

He shrugged. "Just the way I was. Folks called me Bad Boon and that I was—born bad, raised bad, just plain bad—though I wasn't yet an outlaw. One time, after I tangled with a fellow in town, instead of getting tossed in the hoosegow, I got offered a job. A feller from the C. Bain & Company thought I'd make a good guard for the mail. Had me riding shotgun on one of their stages next day. Man, you ain't lived until you've sat on top of a stage behind a team of eight running full out."

He gazed at the water for a while then came back around, glancing to her. She smiled and nodded, silently encouraging him to continue.

"I got pretty good with that rifle. They gave me one and this hat." He patted the brim, still beside him on the bank. "I wanted black, but they only had gray."

"It's a handsome hat."

He ran a finger over the stiff felt of the upturned brim. "Riding guard made me feel important, though it was mostly mail, magazines, parcels and such. They never carried money and advertised as much to try to cut down on robberies. Nobody called me Bad Boon then and I stopped fighting. We outrun a few outlaws. My driver was Ralph Corragan. He was eight years older. He said if I kept out of fights, I'd be a driver soon with a driver's pay. He had a wife and two kids, young ones, not even walking yet."

Laurie noticed that he spoke of Ralph in the past tense and the anticipation of bad news made her queasy.

"He even taught me how to hold the reins when the way was straight and he held my gun. He was holding it the day Hammer's gang attacked the stage. They shot Ralph in the belly, two shots. The blood was dark and there was a lot of it. Those shots were meant for me. I was the guard, not Ralph."

Laurie failed to suppress her shiver.

"He was the first real friend I ever had. I don't much like to get close to folks because of things like that."

"Did the shot kill him?"

Boon shook his head, his lips pressing into

a thin line and his restless fingers closed into fists.

"There were too many and I wasn't a good driver. They surrounded us. I pulled up, because I didn't know what would happen next. I never met a man as ruthless as George Hammer."

Laurie thought of how Boon had ridden their horses until they staggered and knew he had learned of Hammer's ruthlessness through hard experience.

"If I'd known, I'd have driven those horses to death rather than stop. But Ralph was hurt. He could barely hold on. I was afraid he'd fall. So..." He motioned to pull an imaginary brake.

Laurie watched him with wide, nervous eyes. Was she sorry she'd started this train? If she wasn't, she soon would be, Boon thought. He planned to tell her everything. Then she'd know what he was and that would be best for them both, because the way she looked at him sometimes gave him crazy ideas. It got him thinking he might just run off with her and make a home for them. He could work and she could mind their children, teach them to read. He'd like to have boys and girls who knew how to read and cipher. As if Laurie would have him, but she did have the look of a woman who wanted what a man could give her. That's why she needed to know exactly the kind of man he was. Bad Boon, bad through and through.

He met her eyes, holding them without mercy as he told her what came next.

"First thing they did was shoot the passengers. Two women schoolteachers and a Baptist preacher headed for El Paso to start a school. Shot him first, shot him in the face and one of the women in the breast. The last in the back when she tried to run."

Laurie huddled in upon herself as her eyes went round as a horned owl's. She held a hand over her mouth to keep from screaming.

"I was holding Ralph in my arms when they came at me. When they got close, I drew my pistol and aimed it at Hammer. I should have shot him and died right there. Would have been better."

Laurie removed her hand from her mouth and scowled at him. "Don't say that."

He snorted. She hadn't heard the rest yet and it proved full well that she needed to.

"Hammer ordered his boys to hold fire. He told me that I was fast enough to join his men. I said I'd die first. But they didn't point the gun at me—they pointed it at Ralph and ordered me to my feet."

Boon stopped to wipe the sweat from his face. He could still see Ralph staring up at him, that dark blood leaking out of his mouth.

"They shot him anyway?" she asked.

Boon shook his head. If only they had. Why hadn't he shot Hammer when he'd had the chance?

"No. They ordered me to do it."

She gasped. It was hard to have her know, hard to say the truth that he had not spoken to anyone.

"They told me they'd kill Ralph and then shoot me or I could shoot him and join the gang."

"Oh, no." Her words held shock at the realization of what he had done.

"I didn't want to die. Ralph said he was done for anyway. Blood was coming out his mouth and still leaking from him with each beat of his heart. He was pale as a bedsheet and his lips had gone blue. But he wasn't dead until I put the bullet in his heart and became a murderer like the rest of them."

She inched toward him. "But you had no choice."

He snorted and smiled. "I had a choice.

Made the same one I always do. I picked myself first. He was my friend and I killed him."

He waited for her to condemn him, waited for her to tell him that he turned her stomach or that she hated him.

But, to his surprise, she continued to inch across the bedrock that separated them, advancing with a slow determination and a look in her eyes that kept him from doing what he knew was right. If he was a respectable man—the kind of man she deserved—he'd warn her off, tell her to keep back. Instead Boon waited, letting her come.

"You were placed in a horrific position. But your friend was right—he was dying. Even if there was a doctor waiting, he would not have survived such wounds."

"I ended him. Took him from his wife and his babies. Nobody else—me."

"No. Hammer did that. All you did was end his suffering."

Boon gaped, staring down at Laurie's lovely upturned face marred only by the shiner that now circled purple under her left eye. He had expected censure and received mercy. No wonder he could not keep himself from her. Laurie was not like any woman he'd ever come across. She was compassion, beauty and innocence, all contained in the most appealing package he'd ever seen.

Could she be right?

He shook his head, refusing the clemency she offered.

"You're not an outlaw," she insisted, inches closer now.

"I rode with them."

"They held a pistol to your head. You would have left at the first chance, had the opportunity arisen."

"Opportunity? I left them because your father's partner shot my horse out from under me."

"Did you have any occasion to leave them before that? Tell me you had a chance to run and you didn't take it and I'll believe every harsh word you have uttered."

He couldn't because he hadn't. Hammer and his men had watched him like a captive, especially on the one robbery he'd gone on. They wouldn't even give him a gun. He'd been without a gun when her father had captured him. It was one of the captain's questions, why he didn't have a weapon. But he did, that small derringer in his vest pocket. He could have used it to kill Hammer at any time. But he knew that if he did, he'd never get out alive.

Laurie waited, chin raised, certain in her own judgment. At last she nodded. "You see? I knew it. You're a good man, but you just can't see it."

Laurie was wrong. She saw the man he wished he could be, not the man he was.

"I've seen you take great risks to get me out. You kept George Hammer from hitting me. You saved me from the others. If you're so unscrupulous, why did you do all that?"

"Your father sent me."

"I know that. But why you? If he thought you were so wicked, he wouldn't have chosen you."

"I'm the only one who could get past the sentries. Anyone else shows up and they shoot you first."

Her eyes rounded, but her recovery was fast. If he blinked, he'd have missed it.

"I understand why my father sent you. I don't understand why you agreed to come. Did my father offer to pay you?"

"He gave me these." He rested his hands on the twin pistols, seated in the holsters that she now noted looked rather new.

She glanced from his holsters to him and then shook her head. "That wasn't pay. That was arming you for the job. Did he offer a reward for my return?"

He shook his head. His stomach twisted now. She was getting dangerously close to the truth. He should have anticipated this. Laurie was too damned smart for her own good.

"No reward, yet you went in, risked your life and got me out."

Boon retrieved the skillet and his hat. "We ain't out yet."

She followed him to his feet and waved a finger at him. "Oh, no, you don't. You're not done yet. They shot your horse and they didn't hang you, which is very unlike the Rangers."

"Coats wanted me to be hanged."

"I'm sure. Yet they didn't. My father saw something in you. I see it, too. You're the only one who doesn't know that you're a hero."

"That's wrong."

Laurie gnawed her lower lip. If he was a hero, he wouldn't be thinking of kissing her again.

"Then what's in this for you?" she asked.

"Nothing." *Redemption,* he thought and glanced away and felt her hand clamp on his arm.

"He didn't promise you anything. You didn't ask for anything?"

He shook his head.

"But you're hoping for something. Something important. Something you won't have otherwise. You bring me home and my father is indebted to you. What is it he can give you?"

Boon's face heated and he looked away. Laurie gasped.

"You want to be a Texas Ranger!" Her jaw dropped open at the startling discovery. Boon wanted to be a lawman, protect the weak, uphold the law. She blinked in astonishment.

His eyes narrowed and his features hardened into a nasty scowl. He tugged his arm free. "They don't let outlaws into the Rangers."

She ignored that. "But that proves my point. A good man. I knew it all along."

"Laurie, you're crazy. I don't want to…" But he couldn't finish. He wanted it so bad he could feel the weight of that silver star on his shirt. He could see it flash in the sun. He could feel the ache over wanting to belong to that elite group of fighters whose business was to keep folks safe from marauders and rustlers and raiding Apache. Important, dangerous, satisfying work. Work that could make a man proud.

He met her eyes, glaring now, hating her for seeing through him. "Have I thought about it?

Yeah. Along with a lot of other things that I'll never have, like parents, a real home and the love of a good woman."

That last one made her mouth snap shut like a wolf trap.

He forged on. "From where I stand I'll be damned lucky to get out of this alive. The rest is gravy."

Boon was on his feet, stooping to retrieve his hat. Laurie scrambled to join him, frightened by his expression and the hard glint in his eyes. This was how he'd looked when he faced that man and fought him to the death. Her insides trembled at the terrible visage and the stranger now standing before her.

"Do you know why your pa was nice to me? Why he saved me from that noose? It sure wasn't because he felt the need to reform my sorry ass. He needed me to get to you. That's all. He's using me to get you and I'm using him to clear my name. Once that's done he'll cut me loose and I'll take my new pistols and ride for Mexico."

"You could have done that already. You didn't have to come for me."

Boon leaned in, but she didn't back up. He pressed on his hat, left her there beside the stream and stormed up the rock. He paused at the fire but only to scatter the coals with a vicious kick.

"Outlaws don't become Rangers. I'll see you safe and be on my way. Don't you think I won't."

Chapter Ten

"Boon! Wait!" Laurie scurried after him, but he was a man with a purpose and his angry stride took him out of her sight before she could catch him.

She found him at the horses, saddle and blanket in hand, approaching the bay, who slept so soundly he didn't know he was saddled until the blanket contacted his back.

Boon stooped to retrieve the girth that now dangled on the other side of the horse's flank.

"I think you'd make a fine Ranger."

He snorted.

"You saved me," she reminded him, reaching to rest a hand upon his shoulder. Then, thinking better of the action, she let her arm drop back to her side.

He cinched the girth and turned to retrieve the other saddle. The chestnut's ears swiveled as Boon approached. The gelding sidestepped his hindquarters, but Boon barely slowed as he threw the saddle into place.

"Men overcome a difficult past all the time. You can, too. No one has a perfect situation, after all."

He turned on her. "Don't they? What about you, Laurie Bender? You got any secrets? You made any mistakes? Besides last night, I mean."

She felt her ears tingle at that and turned half away, reconsidering her approach. This was a topic she was not willing to discuss with anyone.

"Right," he said and went about bridling the bay.

"I just thought you might like to discuss this."

He paused, the buckle of the throat latch half done, and glanced back at her. "Discuss? Is that what this is—a discussion? Because I spilled my guts back there and you're closed up tighter than an oyster. You dress like a lady and ride like a man and you keep your cards closer to your vest than a riverboat gambler."

She felt herself growing smaller. "I was just

trying to help," she whispered, her voice now tiny and weak.

"I ain't asked your advice, have I?"

Boon completed the buckle and then left the reins to dangle as he headed for the chestnut. She said nothing as he set the saddlebags in place and returned for her.

"Can't afford to tarry. Horses are dry. Time to move."

He extended his hand to assist her but she lifted her leg and gained a footing in the long stirrup, swinging up unaided, then adjusted her long skirts to cover her legs and much of the horse's rump, thoroughly sorry she had tried to comfort him at all.

All too soon they were trotting up the incline in twilight, counting the hours until she could rest. As the trail rose above the stream she opted to clutch the bay's black mane to keep from sliding backward over the cantle. It seemed, at times, she lay half on the creature's neck. They did not reach the canyon rim before the darkness settled over the land. The horses were heaving with the exertion of the steep trail, their sides lathered and their heads hanging.

Boon pulled up and Laurie and the horse both groaned.

"We'll rest here until the moon is up. Then head on," he said.

The landscape was forbidding, all rock and little vegetation. Laurie thought it a horrible place to rest, but said nothing as she drew one tired leg from the stirrup.

Laurie managed to get her leg over the back of the saddle. Boon guided her to the ground and held her about the waist until she had her balance. She smiled wearily at him.

"Thank you."

He gathered the horses' reins and took them down a steep incline to the stream, and she followed behind, twice landing on her backside. Laurie moved upstream to drink as the horses pawed and slurped at the water below her. Boon waited until the horses had their fill and then drank, as well. Making it up the incline was easier for Laurie than the horses, but all found their way to the top of the ridge. There were no trees here, just large rock formations, sculpted by the wind. Boon led them away from the animal path and into the cover of rock, pausing when they were out of sight from anyone pursuing them.

"We've got some time to rest before moonrise." He laid the saddles side by side then set the saddle blankets before them and stretched a bedroll over both.

She collapsed upon the bedding, wearier than ever in her life. Her legs felt weak as water and trembled from the long ride. Boon hobbled the horses.

"I got to go cover our tracks," he said.

Laurie began to rise. "Shall I come with you?"

He shook his head. "Rest awhile. I'll be back directly. I'll whistle like this so you know it's me." He gave a very respectable imitation of the cry of a hawk.

"Hawks don't fly at night," she said.

"Well, I do a poor owl." He favored her with his lopsided smile and headed off.

She watched him go, until he was no more than a shadow moving along the rock face. Had he forgiven her?

The stars shone with just enough light for her to make out her direct surroundings. She wondered how Boon could even see their trail. Peepers began their chorus. Bats flitted overhead, diving and darting after insects, dark silhouettes against the star-scattered sky.

Laurie waited. Her eyes grew heavy. She thought the bats might not notice her if she was lower to the ground, so she rested her head on one of the saddles.

She stared up at the stars and wondered if her father and his men were already waiting at the station. She did not understand when it happened, but it seemed that overnight she went from the freedom of a girl riding over the rolling hills with her father, to a woman packaged in taffeta bonnets, ribbons and bows. After that, he was away more than he was home. Every time he did return, her parents fought, always about the same thing: the raising of Laurie. Her father wanted his wife and child nearby; Mother insisted on living in a city, away from Indians and rustlers. She said the wilderness was no place to raise their daughter. His visits became less frequent, then he stopped coming altogether and her mother had filed for divorce. Recently her mother began seeing a man named Calvin.

Laurie stared up at the twinkling stars and thought about what Boon had said, about her father saving him so he could rescue his daughter. It didn't make sense.

A moment later, she heard the cry of a hawk and sat up as Boon appeared from the darkness. He came to sit beside her, his features shrouded by the night.

"When were you captured by the Rangers?" she asked.

"Three weeks back."

"But, Boon, my father couldn't have known I would be captured back then or he would have prevented it."

Boon turned, his mind perhaps picking up the inconsistency she had detected.

"When he spared you, he did not do so because he needed you to rescue me. So there must be some other reason."

"Well, if he had one, I can't think what it was."

"Perhaps he found you to be truthful and brave and wanted you to have a second chance. If that is the case, I hope you will use that chance to pursue your calling."

He snorted. "You forget where I come from."

"That never determines where a man will go. Look at Abraham Lincoln. He came from humble roots."

Boon stared at her as if she'd gone mad. "You think I'm up for being president?"

She nodded. "If you chose to be. But what is more important is what you want." She gave him a pointed look.

"Lincoln never killed no one."

"I believe that many in the South would disagree with you there."

"Why is it every time we get talking it's about me. Let's talk about you for a change."

"Presently," she said, steering the conversation back to him. "I think you should become a Ranger, if that is what you wish to be."

"Easy to say." He leaned back on the saddle beside hers, using it as a backrest. Then he tipped his hat back so he could gaze up at the stars, emerging like silver fish rising to the surface of a dark pool until the sky was littered with them.

Boon folded his arms across his chest and let his body ease back. It felt good to stretch out and it felt good to sit quietly beside Laurie.

"Is that what you want?" she asked.

He hesitated and then gave in. Why not tell her? What difference did it make? And if she wanted to laugh, then let her.

"Always fancied being a lawman. When those range bums got loco in town and the bar dog couldn't handle them, it was the sheriff who kept order. He took care of the girls even though they was just…well, he did his job the same whether you was the mayor's daughter or a good-time girl. Once a couple of Rangers came into the house. Never seen one before, but boy howdy, did they get everyone's attention. Bought them drinks. Best of everything. I knew that day what I wanted. Didn't seem impossible back then."

"That's why you rode for the stage. You wanted to protect people."

His head sank. "And I failed."

"Oh, Boon, you were outnumbered and set upon by an outlaw who had evaded capture from many more experienced fighters than you."

"Still burns me up inside."

"And well it should. That's the kind of fire that makes you do better the next time."

"Next time? Laurie, you sure have an optimistic nature."

"No, I have a selfish nature."

"How you figure?"

"You said I never speak of myself, but that is because what I have to say is not very flattering. This, for instance. I came out here to find my father in order to urge him to stop my mother from remarrying a very sweet, honorable man because that was what was best for me. I hate being the child of a divorce. The ladies in town avoid my mother and their sons avoid me. I thought it was because of the divorce, but lately I have begun to wonder." She clasped her hands over her abdomen and went silent so long, Boon thought she'd finished just about the time she started up again. "But my mother is content with Calvin. They don't fight and he is there with her every day, unlike my father who is chasing all over Texas after outlaws, Indians and thieves. Still, I wanted to stop them and *that* is selfish."

Boon removed his hat and settled down so his head rested on the seat of his saddle. "That don't seem so bad."

"If I had stayed home, none of this would have happened." She met his gaze. "But then again, I never would have met you."

His answer was immediate and harsh. "That's no loss."

"You're wrong, Boon. You are, without question, the best thing that has happened to me in years. I know you will protect me from them. I trust you."

"*You* trust *me?*" he asked. His voice no longer held the venom he'd kindled before leaving the waterfall. Something about her nearness stole his irritation. His heart began a slow increase, building beat by beat.

"With my life," she said, rolling toward him and clasping her strong little hands around his upper arm. The heat made his blood race so fast he felt light-headed. "And I think you would make a fine Texas Ranger."

He cocked his head and stared at her, her face a wash of blue in the starlight. Then he shrugged an arm about her, drawing her close, hugging her against his side. Laurie rolled toward him and pressed herself against him. He breathed in the warm familiar scent of her body and took comfort in her soft contours. His arms came about her and he rested his cheek upon her head.

"Oh, Laurie, you sure do have bad taste in men."

"I do not," she murmured. "You are the bravest man I have ever met."

"Your father is braver."

"He likely would have set me on a horse and told me to ride north while he went after Hammer." She drew back, looping her arms about his neck and toying with the hairs at his collar, making the skin on his neck tingle. "You would never do that. No one has ever put me first before."

Boon stiffened. "Laurie, I'm not your sweetheart."

"I know that. But you have been kind and you have defended me. And when we kissed—"

He cut her off. "Laurie, I won't lie. I fancy you. But you're the captain's daughter and I know my duty."

"That would not stop some."

"Well, I'm not some. I told you about my ma. I seen firsthand how it is with women. Life can be hard."

His words only proved to her that she was right about him. Laurie let his soft blond hair slide between her fingers.

How different he was from other men, flirting, teasing, trying to steal a kiss or lure her into some private corner. Until Boon, she had never wanted to be touched that way. But with him she discovered the true meaning of desire. She respected him and fancied him and wanted him to kiss her again, perhaps do more than kiss her. She felt that same jolt of longing fluttering in her heart.

Boon captured the hand that raked his hair and brought it away from his neck. "I'm bringing you back just like I found you, untouched."

Untouched.

The stab of sorrow pierced her like a bullet. Laurie pressed her lips together to keep him from seeing the quavering of her chin, and failed. He couldn't know that this was already impossible and she would not tell him.

"What is it?"

Her charade came crashing down about her like a glass house. She shook her head in denial—if she just kept pretending, it would be all right. It had to be.

But now she faced a new dilemma. She was all mixed-up when it came to Boon. She wanted him, but did not want him to know of her condition. She wanted to appear proper while longing to be kissed. He said he would bring her home untouched, but what would he do if he knew that was already impossible?

He knelt before her now, gripped her shoulders. She couldn't meet his eyes.

"Did one of Hammer's men take you before you got to camp?"

She shook her head.

"Laurie, are you sure?"

She lifted her chin, peeking at him, her hands locked over her face, which burned at what she was about to reveal, the truth she'd hidden for so long. The realization both terrified and beckoned. She only now recognized how heavy the burden of that secret had become. But she would lay it down now, give it to Boon.

"Not at camp," she managed, her words sticking like flies on syrup.

"Where?" His tone had turned deadly.

"It's bad," she whispered.

He released her, his hand stroking down her upper arms as he pulled away. Boon crossed his hands over one upturned knee and waited. "Whatever it is, I've done worse. You can tell me." He waited but she kept her head down. "You said you trusted me, Laurie. If that's true, you'll tell me."

She did trust him. But it would be hard to let him see her as she truly was—a liar who had ruined herself before she had even become a woman. The facade she'd created to cover the truth crumbled.

Laurie's throat grew tight and her eyes burned. Tears were coming and squeezing her eyelids tight and pressing her lips together would not contain them.

She knew what she was and soon Boon would know, as well, because she already knew she was going to tell him everything. She was going to divulge what she had shared with no one, and the realization frightened her to the core.

Laurie lifted her chin and told him her secret.

"You can't bring me home untouched, Boon. It's already too late for that. I was ruined before they ever captured me." She covered her mouth with her hand and grabbled with her uneven breathing as the regret ripped around inside her.

"What?"

The disbelief showed in his eyes first. She said nothing more as she watched the incredulity harden into acceptance. What was he thinking?

She lowered her hand. "I let a man have me. It was a mistake, but I'm still ruined."

"No. You're not."

His adamant tone made Laurie's breath catch. Boon looked angry, but to her astonishment he was not angry with her.

"Laurie, lying with a man does not mark you. Any man who chooses a woman for her purity is a fool and not worthy of you."

She pulled back to stare at him, wanting to believe him. Knowing that Boon didn't think like other men. A gentleman wanted a pure wife who had only known his touch.

"That's not true," she whispered, wishing it were. Wishing she could find a man who really believed such nonsense.

"It is, because innocence is temporary. You can't hold on to it any more than you can keep your baby teeth. Any man worth his salt knows to choose a woman for who she is inside. Not for the color of her hair or a silly hat or even for her pretty face. Those things don't last."

"Most men would disagree with you."

"Laurie, you're tough enough to survive Hammer's camp and riding all night and day. That tells me you are tough enough to get through this, and you're kind. You haven't judged me like everyone else I've ever met. I'm telling you that you don't need your innocence. You don't. Any man would still want you."

"Any man?" she asked.

He hesitated, his answer filled with both caution and conviction. "Yes."

"Then prove it."

"What?"

"Prove that I'm still desirable even though I've been used by another man. Prove to me that you can overlook it." She angled her chin and threw him a challenge with her eyes. "Kiss me again."

George Hammer led his men up the box canyon. Furlong and Freet had found the tracks of his quarry, but it had taken too damned long. The rabbits had a few hours' head start. Still, he was riding with a woman, a white woman who was unaccustomed to rough travel. He'd be surprised if Laurie Bender had ever sat a horse before. Most ladies didn't.

It had been Freet who recognized the tracks, even in the dark, because one of the horses had thrown a shoe and Freet had seen it glinting by moonlight.

George hoped the canyon led nowhere. He'd love to trap Boon against a cliff and use him for target practice. Bastard, sneaking into camp and stealing from him.

"Hold," called Freet.

George urged his horse forward. He never rode point, just in case of ambush.

"What's wrong?" he growled, his fury now contained in a pressing need for vengeance. They must be close.

Freet dismounted, taking the lantern from Furlong, then ran along the ground like a bloodhound, lantern raised.

"Freet lost the trail," said Furlong, sneering at his fellow.

"Think you can do better?" growled Hammer. "Get off your damned horse and help him look."

They'd lost their tracks once before at a fork, but they'd find Boon, because Hammer would not be denied the pleasure of killing him. He already anticipated what he'd do. Maybe over a fire, like the Comanche raiders once did. Yes, he'd enjoy seeing Boon's flesh blister. Or slice off his eyelids and leave him staked to the ground to await the sun's torture.

And as for Laurie…

George had never planned on letting her live. The only thing that Captain Bender would get in exchange for the reward was his daughter's corpse.

"Campfire," called Freet, from somewhere in the brush.

"Still hot?" asked Hammer.

Chapter Eleven

Boon's insides stung as if they were cut from swallowed glass. He'd never felt like this—worried, protective, helpless. But Laurie was talking crazy. He knew what would happen if he kissed her again.

Did she?

She lifted her pointed chin, staring up at him, her eyes dark as the far side of the moon. Something inside him flipped and tightened. He wanted to hold this woman to his heart forever.

He saw his need reflected back to him in her dark eyes. This was not the look he'd expected. He'd thought to find her in need of comfort. But this was not the kind of comfort he'd thought she'd need. One look told him he'd been mistaken. Laurie had transformed herself into a woman of a certain mind. Her stare was direct, bold, her lips parted and her eyelids half-hooded. This was a woman demanding to be kissed.

He didn't believe it. But his body reacted, his pulse galloping along like an eight-horse team. He battled for control of his impulses, even as he felt himself surging like a runaway horse.

"Laurie?"

"Boon, if what you say is true then you'll kiss me. I want you to touch me again. I want to feel that again, but this time I want to touch you, too."

He drew a breath at the image her words conjured. Now he wasn't on horseback. Now he could easily take her. He'd planned their first encounter but the pull between them had been so strong that he was dead sure he would have taken her if he could have. Now she wanted him again and he'd have to give her what she needed and keep from taking what he wanted.

"Not a good idea, Laurie. I want you too much. I could, I might..." Words failed him. If he spoke, if he mentioned an unwanted pregnancy, she might change her mind. *Lord, please don't let her change her mind.*

He was a hypocrite. Hadn't he just told her he would never take a woman without wedding her first? But Laurie didn't want a husband, or, at least, she did not want a husband like him.

But she did want his body and she wanted the proof of his words—that even knowing what she'd done he still found her desirable.

She bit her lower lip and seeing her white teeth draw across the full, plump flesh drove him to madness. His breathing came fast, as if he ran and needed the extra air, yet he lay still as a river rock.

He couldn't do this.

If he cared about her, he'd see she got what she wanted, a husband she could be proud of. Her father had left him in charge of his only daughter. He had to bring her home safe.

Laurie lifted a hand to his chest and gripped his shirt in her fist, pleading with her eyes.

He hesitated. Her eyes went cold.

"I knew it," she said, her hands slipping from him.

Boon seized her up in his arms, capturing her against him.

Desire flared in her eyes as she recognized she had won. Her breathing was labored and the rise and fall of her breasts against the sheer cotton of her blouse made his skin tingle all over.

She wore a blouse, chemise, skirt, stockings…and nothing else.

He rose up to his knees and took hold of her, bringing her into his arms. He could feel her breath on his cheek, her soft breasts pressing against his chest and her fingers raking his back. Needy little moans came from her throat and he had not even kissed her yet. But he would. He closed his eyes at the realization that he was willing to set aside everything he believed to have her just once.

It was all he'd ever get of her. He knew it, and the truth tasted bitter in his mouth. Laurie was like an angel fallen to earth. Any moment the heavens would snatch her up again and she'd be lost to him forever.

But tonight she was his. He closed his eyes, offering a prayer of thanks and a plea for forgiveness. He'd never taken a woman, never longed for a woman, until Laurie. Somehow, she stripped him of all his principles and left him with nothing but need.

She tipped her head back, offering herself to him, and he slanted his mouth over hers. Her lips were soft and pliant. He pulled her even tighter. Boon ran his tongue over her upper lip, tasting the sweetness of her skin. She gasped and he took the opportunity to slip his tongue into her mouth.

He recalled their first kiss, before the outlaws, when Laurie had kissed him back. When she'd pulled away, he saw the horror and the shame. He hoped never to see such a look upon her sweet face again. Did she know what she was doing this time or was she also chased by madness?

He tried to draw back, to see if she had changed her mind before he lost his completely, but she threaded her fingers in his hair and tugged, bringing him closer.

So she wanted more than a kiss. He didn't know why. Didn't care why.

He let his hands roam up and down the twin columns that flanked her spine; strong, firm muscles greeted his exploration. On the third descent, he tugged her blouse clear of her skirts and let his hands run up the chemise until he felt the soft, warm flesh of her shoulders. She pressed against him, sighed and then twisted, as if offering him access to the long row of tiny buttons. He began at the hem and worked north. She did not hinder him, but lay back in his arms, tugging his shirttails free and working his buttons with swift, efficient movements. She finished first and reached with greedy hands, stroking his chest with featherlight caresses. He closed his eyes at the magic of her touch.

He was more than ready for her, but he wanted this to be perfect. He would not rush. He'd show the control he hoped would allow them both to experience the ultimate pleasure together, the way he'd been told it could happen by his teacher, Paulette.

Her mouth was on his skin, kissing and licking. He groaned as he directed her mouth to his chest, holding her head against him. She hesitated only an instant before drawing his nipple into her mouth. The tug and draw sent an electric charge of sweet desire bolting through him, increasing his readiness and his need.

He startled into motion, plucking her from him and turning her so he could kiss the pale column of her neck, nuzzle against the soft lobe of her ear and place kisses over her closed lids. He drew the blouse open, revealing the swell of her breasts above the top of her chemise. She tugged at the pink ribbon that held this final barrier over her shoulders, shrugged from her blouse and pulled the chemise down to expose her breasts. Then she sighed, relaxing back against the saddle. The smell of leather mixed with her sweet scent of lavender.

He had seen her in the sunlight, naked and free. But this was different. Then she had been joyful and relaxed. Now her breathing was labored and her expression strained. The lovely orbs of her breasts lay naked before him like a feast and her pale skin seemed blue in the starlight.

He stared at her, mantled in the shadows of the night. If only he were a painter he could render her perfection, capturing her beauty for all time. Instead, he reached for her.

She offered her mouth. The moment their lips touched she melted against him. Warm, soft flesh pressed to his. She was small, curvy and soft as a rabbit's pelt.

He pulled her close. She exhaled the breath she held in a long sigh. If she'd let him, he would give her all the pleasure he knew how to give.

Laurie stretched out against him again. He ran one finger up the center of her chest. She shivered and writhed. He longed to cup her breast, but he'd not go too fast again. He made wide circles around the full orbs, caressing, stroking, until she arched up and reached for him, bringing one of his hands to a breast and pressing it tight.

He smiled and dipped to kiss her, as he pinched the budded nipple and heard her gasp against his mouth.

"So sweet," he whispered. "I could eat you up."

"Just like the big, bad wolf," she murmured, her eyes shut, her head back.

He laid her down upon his blanket and leaned over her. He nuzzled her and stroked. She hiked up her skirts and he glimpsed the flash of white thighs. She splayed her legs and the sight of her, lying open and waiting for him, sent a surge of need roaring through his system like a locomotive.

She tugged at his flapping shirt, and he kissed her again. His mind reeled. Laurie's fingers scored his back, ran over his chest and belly. He threw one leg between hers, nudging her thighs wider apart. He rested on his side with access to all of her. She let him stroke her breasts and caress the warm damp places between her thighs.

She arched and moaned and tossed her head. He felt himself descending to mindlessness, losing control. He settled between her legs, positioning himself to take her.

Laurie felt Boon's body pressing her to the earth, but still it wasn't enough. She needed to be closer, needed to feel him everywhere. She tossed and plunged and arched, like a ship caught in rough seas, urging him on. His fingers danced over the wetness and touched that lightning rod of sensation between her legs. She felt the familiar building tension that told her she climbed toward bliss.

Now she felt the hard male part of him, pressing against her thigh. And unlike that first time, she wanted him—no, needed him—to come inside her. She reached, splaying her fingers over his buttocks, and pressed, demanding what she desired.

He knelt, the weight of his upper body held on one strong extended arm as he positioned himself at her cleft. She looked up at him and saw his grim features, the bunching of his jaw and the seriousness of his lowered brow. He hesitated.

Was he waiting for her?

It shocked her. Boon clearly wanted this, yet he held back. The cost was the trembling of his body. He reminded her of the racehorses she'd seen, quivering in anticipation as they waited for the pistol shot signal to run.

She nodded her head, giving her consent.

He closed his eyes in relief and began his entrance, slowly, as if she were made of glass. Farther and farther he slipped, the lovely friction driving her mad.

His eyes opened and widened as he thrust all the way inside her, unhindered by the tissue that would prove to a husband she was intact.

This time there was no pain, no tearing. Instead the sensation was exquisite. Laurie gasped and lifted her hips, bringing him even tighter against her. He began to move now, but not in a jerking contortion. Oh, no, Boon's moves were fluid, arousing. The glide and thrust stole her breath and then he withdrew and she reached to capture him, but he was back again, his hips thrusting as his stomach tightened, using all that muscle and sinew to drive her mad.

She threw her head back to savor each wonderful glide, feeling the bubble inside her stretching and straining as it searched for release. He moved faster, she met each stroke with one of her own.

The bubble burst and she shattered, losing her thoughts, her fears, her hopes. Everything disappeared as she rode the bucking waves of sheer sensation—bliss.

From a distance she heard him cry her name

and then he was falling upon her, his weight bringing her back safely to earth. He rolled away, lying beside her as they panted and trembled. The cool, dry air drew the moisture from her skin and a pleasant lethargy stole through her body like a drug. Her eyes drifted closed and she nestled against Boon, clutching his strong right arm and using his biceps as a pillow. He wrapped that arm about her and dragged her closer, letting her head fall on his chest. He stroked her long hair as a chorus of peepers sang them to sleep.

Laurie's last thought was that she wished she could lie here in his arms forever.

Boon roused when the moonlight touched his face. Time to ride again. His body had stiffened and his arm was all pins and needles. He started to stretch and then realized that Laurie lay against him, her blouse unbuttoned, her skirts all a tangle.

It came back to him in a rush of shame and remorse. He'd done it. He'd taken Laurie.

The next thought knocked against his sleep-dulled brain. There was none of the expected resistance described to him by Paulette and no blood. Laurie had told him the truth. She really had not been a virgin.

Why wasn't Laurie a virgin?

Gradually new concerns wiggled to life. He'd taken Laurie to his bed. He'd allowed her to cajole him into breaking his vow because when faced with the choice of having Laurie out of wedlock and never having Laurie at all, he'd taken the easy road—again.

He placed his free hand on his forehead, closing his eyes, feeling nauseous. He'd never bedded a woman, though he'd done everything else to Paulette, including kissing her between the thighs. The boys said it wasn't natural not to take a woman and he'd come to a bad end unless he found a willing gal. Could they have been right? He was like Texas, suffering the worst droughts on record, and Laurie was a rainmaker. He couldn't resist her.

He had promised himself that he'd never do such a thing to a woman. What was he made of that he fell into the first real temptation set in his path? But Laurie was more than that, surely. And she'd been willing, no, eager to have him.

He beat the heel of his hand against his forehead. It didn't matter what she wanted. It didn't matter what she said. Because it was *his* job to do the right thing and that included keeping his damned mitts off.

He'd taken a woman, not his wife, and he'd enjoyed it more than he'd enjoyed anything in his entire life.

He'd lost complete control of himself and that meant there could be a baby. Laurie could lose everything or be railroaded into a bad marriage all because of what he had done. Would her father force him to wed her? The spark of hope that glowed inside him made him sick. Had he done this on purpose, hoping to drive her to him?

If she had a child, she might be his. The hungry part of his mind instantly responded. He wanted her to have his child, wanted her linked to him forever. That way, she'd have to accept him, wouldn't she?

The thought shamed him. It was the woman who trapped the man with such a trick. He'd never heard of the reverse, but if it would get him Laurie…

No.

He ought to be horsewhipped. What kind of man was he to take a woman while she was under his protection?

Certainly not the kind that would ever wear a star. And not the sort of man a father would choose for his girl. Boon felt his insides harden to stone as he recognized he'd never have a

Ranger's star and he'd never keep Laurie. He'd have a better chance of running for governor than winning either one.

Beside him, Laurie's breathing changed, but she settled back to slumber. Wrung out. She wasn't used to outlaw camps or night riding or having a man throw her skirts up over her head.

As if roused by his attention, Laurie startled, opened her eyes, blinked up at the bright perfect half-moon shining down on her face, making it ghostly white except for the dark bruise on her cheek. His insides twisted up like a wood shaving seeing what Hammer had done to her. Knowing he'd done worse.

He watched the confusion knit her brow and then the wash of remembrance as her dark eyes grew so large he could see the white all the way around the iris. She exhaled, squeezing her eyes shut, as if trying to force back the recollection of what had happened to her since she left her mother's arms.

He did not think he could feel any worse until he saw her turn away.

What had he expected, that she'd be happy to find a snake in her bed?

Chapter Twelve

Laurie felt Boon lying beside her, heard his breathing. The stillness and tension told her he was not asleep. Oh, what had she done? The last time she had been cajoled, coerced and persuaded. But not this time. This time she had begged him for it.

Sleeping with Boon hadn't proved to her that her past didn't mark her. It had only revealed to him exactly what kind of a woman she was.

She kept her hands at her side, knowing he stared at her, wishing she could cover her eyes, wishing she could disappear, wishing she could continue to pretend she was a lady, and not a…a…

She turned her head away.

Her wanton behavior had unmasked her. She was not and would never be that ivory, self-contained, respectable pillar of the community.

What would become of her? She pictured herself hanging over a balcony, shouting lewd comments to potential customers. What else was there for a woman who could not keep from letting a man take her right out here in the open?

She'd escaped Hammer. They were on the run. But even the danger of pursuit could not keep her from revealing her baser instincts.

He reached for her. She stiffened but allowed him to gather her up. He rocked her back and forth.

"Are you grieved?" he asked.

"It was wonderful," she admitted. "I never knew it could feel like that. But it's still wrong, isn't it?"

It didn't feel wrong to him. Everything about Laurie felt just right. "I dunno."

"You really think it doesn't matter?"

He knew what she asked. It did matter, deeply, but not for the reasons she believed. He cared because her past scarred her and that made him mad.

"You got to quit blaming yourself."

"But I let him."

"Did you or did he take advantage of you?"

She pressed closer, speaking into his chest as she nestled beside his heart.

"Why don't you tell me exactly what happened. Let me shoulder it for a while."

Oh, how she wanted to. Boon gave her a little squeeze and the words poured from her.

"I held this secret so long and so hard it's a wonder it didn't choke me to death. Shamed me to the very core and still shames me. I was such a fool." She met his eye again and didn't look away as she spoke, her voice now heavy with resignation. "He was one of my father's men. He told me not to tell anyone and I was fool enough to do as he asked. I found out later that he was already seeing the woman he married at the same time he took me out riding. I felt so stupid for believing him when he said he cared and for letting him do that to me." Laurie glanced out into the night, her gaze taking her to some other time and place. Her voice had a faraway quality when she next spoke. "He didn't see me again and I was glad. Then my mother told me he had up and married Gail Hampton. I avoided him, but he sought me out and he said if I told anyone it would be worse for me than for him. That no decent man would want me if they knew. And it's true. I've been so afraid."

Boon listened with a sorrow and a rising rage at what had happened to Laurie.

"That man is a scoundrel."

"And I'm a fool. I never told. I was so afraid my parents would turn me out."

"How old were you?"

"Fourteen."

Boon could not prevent the sharp intake of breath and the exhale that was no more than a hiss.

"He was?"

"Nineteen."

"You were a child and no more at fault than a woman who was robbed."

"I could have fought him."

"Fought? No, you shouldn't have to fight. The man was a villain. What's his name?"

That gave her pause.

"Why do you want to know?"

"Tell me, Laurie, or I'll find out some other way."

She hesitated only a moment longer. "Anton Fischer."

"Good." Up until this minute he'd never wanted to kill a man out of revenge. Now he did. He wanted to kill the man who hurt Laurie and he wanted to do it with his bare hands.

But that would have to wait. Right now he had to tell Laurie that his recklessness might result in pregnancy.

Boon rose from their bed and Laurie followed him, her skirts falling demurely about her ankles once more as she turned to fastening the buttons of her blouse.

He knew he was not supposed to speak about such things to a lady. He'd been told you couldn't even mention a woman's legs without offending. So how did he broach this topic without getting his ears pinned back? He decided to go at it fast and hard.

"Laurie, listen to me. I have to tell you something. You might be carrying my child."

Her head jerked up, meeting his gaze while her fingers remained motionless on the top button of her blouse. Her wide eyes showed white in the moonlight.

"I don't understand," she whispered.

She didn't. One look at her startled expression that bordered on panic told him that.

Sweet Lord, didn't they teach girls anything? He thought back to the ones who raised him. Was it possible he knew more about women's business than Laurie did?

"Laurie, what we done, that's how babies come, from a man and a woman, together." He motioned his head back at the ground where they had lain together.

Her hands rose to clasp her cheeks. "What… what do I do?"

"Do? You do nothing. Just wait. If your monthly comes on time, you're clear. You can forget me and what we done and go on and do as you please. If not, well, we got business."

She blinked at him. "Is that how I would know?"

He groaned. Why didn't mothers give their daughters one bit of useful information where men were concerned? Then they wouldn't be such easy prey for unscrupulous men, men like him.

He thought back to the time Lottie got with child, reciting the symptoms from memory. "That's the most important sign. Sometimes you throw up and such and some foods make you queasy, because the baby can make you sick for a time before you start to show."

She covered her eyes with her hands, rocking now, her elbows pressed tight to her sides as if already sick.

He knew she was grieved. Didn't blame her. She'd every right to hate him. She deserved better. He'd failed her and he'd failed her father, the man he'd sought to impress.

Boon gritted his teeth as he retrieved his hat. By dishonoring Captain Bender's daughter, he'd done the one unforgivable thing and would be lucky not to get shot over it.

Coming to a stand, he scrubbed his face with his hands, his spurs jangling as he did so. His head sank. He'd not even taken off his boots. He'd treated her as the cowpunchers treated the women who had raised him—money exchanged, a quick poke and then a hasty goodbye.

Laurie deserved so much better. Lord, he wished he were the man to give it to her.

"I didn't know," she whispered.

She met his eyes now, though her chin now trembled. He stepped forward to take her in his arms, but she retreated so quickly he paused, letting his arms drop back to his sides.

Why was it that everything he said or did with her was wrong?

"I'll stand by you, Laurie."

She lifted a hand so the white of her palm nearly touched his face. "No."

Her quick rejection stung. "You gonna hide this like you hid the other?"

She flapped her hands. "What choice do I have?"

She could marry him. That thought made him sway. As if she ever would. As if the captain would permit such a match. He knew what kind of a man she wanted. Someone rich and respectable.

"Fine. For now we'll wait and see."

Boon glanced up, seeing the silvery halo above the cliff face behind them.

"Moon's up," he said. "I best saddle the horses."

He retrieved one saddle and blanket, then left her by the stream. The horses hadn't gone far. He saddled the little bay who had carried Laurie all day, cinching the girth and replacing the bridle, then looping the reins about a twisted mesquite tree before retracing his steps.

"I'm going to wash my face," she said, sweeping past him toward the stream.

He heard her retreat down the hill, accompanied by the slide of the tiny rocks and gravel and then splashing as she reached the stream. He saddled the second horse and headed after her when his ears picked up another sound, the metallic spin of a spur.

* * *

Laurie left Boon by the horses and hurried toward the stream. She reached the bank, kneeling to wash her face with the cool water.

She pressed her wet hands to her hot face, washing away the tears and the dust and the heartbreak. She thought of what he had told her. She might be with child. His child, the child of an outlaw. If she were, would this new life also be outcast because of what its father was and what she had done? Her parents would certainly disown her. Had this very thing happened to Boon's mother?

Laurie felt as if she were falling down a well deeper and deeper until she was so far down she knew she could never crawl out.

What had they done?

She heard the spin of the rowels of Boon's spurs and turned toward him, bereft and empty as an open grave. She stared at his silhouette. Even in her dark musings she recognized that something was wrong. This man was too short, too stocky to be Boon. She stood in slow motion, clutching the open gap of her shirt, above the chemise against her throat. The scream was there, trapped inside her like a wild bird in a snare. Try as she might she could not release it. Boon, she needed to warn him, needed to run. But her legs seemed fixed to the stone beneath her feet. She was a deer, confronted by the wolf, looking death in the face.

"Hello, Laurie. Hammer's going to be real glad to see you."

She reached for her pistol at the back of her waistband only to remember that she had left it with her saddle. Trembling, she backed away toward the water.

The outlaw advanced, as if in no hurry.

Had he killed Boon? She'd heard no shot, but the killer had a long knife tethered in a sheath at his belt. That thought sent an earthquake of terror through her and she stopped retreating. If he'd harmed Boon she'd see that he paid. She went down on one knee, lifting a flat splinter of the bedrock up in her hand, using her thumb to judge the cutting edge and finding it sharp.

The outlaw glanced about, the blue glint of steel showing from his pistol as he swept the clearing.

"Where's Boon?" he asked.

Laurie had to shut her eyes against the relief. He hadn't killed Boon.

"Here, Freet" came the reply directly behind the intruder.

The outlaw whirled and fired wild at the

same instant Laurie saw the flash of Boon's pistol and heard the second shot. Freet fell to his knees as the gun dropped to his side, then he toppled onto the bedrock.

Boon ran forward, kicking the gun away then turning to Laurie.

She ran to Boon, throwing herself against him. But he took hold of her with only one arm, keeping the other for his pistol as he pulled her against him.

"You hurt?"

She shook her head, then realized he had his eyes on Freet.

"No," she answered. "I thought he killed you."

"He ain't that good. Came clomping up here on horseback. Step away now."

Boon kicked the pistol away and squatted beside Freet, rolling him over. The blood pouring from his chest glistened black in the moonlight.

"Missed his heart. Lung shot." He turned to Freet. "You alone?"

The man nodded.

"How far back?" he asked.

Freet's jaw moved but nothing came from his mouth but frothy, bubbling blood.

Boon grabbed him by his vest and dragged

him into the brush. A moment later Laurie heard Boon say, "That's all the grave you merit, you son of a bitch." He returned to Laurie. "Grab his pistol."

She did, finding the grip still warm. She gathered her clothing, dressing quickly as Boon collected Freet's horse. Laurie carried his full canteen and heavy pistol as they made their way in haste to their horses.

As Boon checked Freet's horse and saddle, he spoke to Laurie. "Freet is a scout. They know which canyon we took and they're behind us. When Freet don't come back, they'll pick up and ride hard."

"The trail is steep behind us."

"That's all the advantage we got."

He left the rest unsaid. They were in trouble and it would be a miracle if they reached the station before they were caught by the Hammer.

"It's because we stopped."

"Had to or kill the horses and we couldn't ride in full dark."

She glanced toward the brush, listening to the wheeze of Freet's last breaths.

"You saved me again," she whispered.

He grimaced. "Laurie, I…"

His words trailed off. He stared at her with

a look of such heartbreak she found herself holding her breath as anxiety coiled inside her.

At last he said, "You ready?"

Laurie exhaled. There was so much she needed to say, but there was no time to say it. She could see from his downcast expression that he blamed himself when she'd all but demanded he kiss her.

And it had been wonderful. With Anton she'd been afraid, inexperienced, alone. Her encounter with Anton had been humiliating. But with Boon, the loving was sweet and wild and full of wonder. If she were honest, she'd admit that she loved it and that made her everything she'd feared she might become.

Boon chose Freet's horse, tying his gelding behind Freet's as she mounted up.

"Once we climb out of this canyon, we're going at a gallop until we make the station or one or all three of these horses drop."

Laurie nodded her understanding and gathered the reins, grateful for her father's lessons on horsemanship.

The next few hours were a blur of motion and changing light. The moon set, casting them in near darkness and slowing their pace to a walk. At last the sky brightened to a deep midnight-blue and she could again see the landscape about them. They were loping along when the sun rose. Her relief at the sun's appearance quickly abated as temperatures rose and the dry heat blazed off rock and canyon.

By midmorning, her mare began to wheeze, her sides glistening with sweat. Boon pulled up to change horses, remounting his chestnut and seating her on Freet's horse, then tying her mare behind.

Perspiration poured off Laurie, as well, rolling down her back and between her breasts. She felt her skin burning in the midday sun for she never went out without both bonnet and parasol. But she had never before ridden for her life.

Finally, they came to a real road, the road from Fort Concho to San Antonio, the road that held the stage station—rarely used any longer now that the railroad stretched from Texarkana all the way to El Paso. But the mail still came through this way, bringing packages periodically to the outlying settlements. She craned her neck but could not see anything past the horse before her and Boon's back, hunched over the neck of his mount. A glance behind showed no sign of pursuit, but black clouds were sweeping in from the south.

Beneath the storm clouds, the gray sheets of rain curtained the road.

Not long afterward, the rumble of thunder reached her and soon after that, Boon began to slow. She spotted the long stable that looked large enough to house a team of six to ten horses. Laurie noticed the squatty little station beyond the stable, also built of adobe bricks without any plaster. The station was a singularly unappealing building that looked like a broken pot butting up against a steep incline. This structure served as a rest stop for passengers and as a residence for the stationmaster. The yard was empty and the stable roof had collapsed in the forward inside corner. Clearly, this structure had seen better days.

She craned her neck for some sign of her father, but no one appeared. The horses pawed at the ground in an anxious motion that echoed the worry now squeezing her heart. Laurie's elation at reaching safety slowly wilted with her smile as the silence stretched. There were no horses, no recent tracks, no greeting, no welcome and no sign that her father and his men were waiting to rescue them.

She glanced toward Boon, standing in his stirrups, his hat pushed back. He seemed frozen in place as his gaze swept their surroundings. His mouth, she noted, had turned to a thin line across his angled face.

The knot in her stomach solidified into a heavy ball of rock-hard dread. No one was here.

"Where are they?" she asked.

Chapter Thirteen

Boon looked about the empty yard before the stage station as the unease built steadily inside him. Beside him, Laurie used her hand as a visor to search for her father.

"Why aren't they here?" she asked.

"Not sure."

Boon's horse staggered as he dismounted. Her mare's head sank and she heaved, white foam frothing from her mouth. Boon helped Laurie down and she found herself equally unsteady as she walked with Boon, who led the horses to the water trough. Once the horses were watered he looped the reins over the hitching post.

"Didn't you say he would meet us here?" Laurie considered for one instant that Boon had lied to her and then dismissed the possibility. She trusted him.

"He did." Boon wondered what had happened. Surely it must be terrible if it kept Captain Bender from being here to protect his daughter. All manner of tragedies played out in his mind.

"Is this the right station?"

Boon nodded, hand on his pistol as he looked about the empty yard. Then he glanced back the way they had come, seeing nothing but the storm sweeping in with astonishing speed.

"We need fresh horses if we're riding on."

Laurie turned to face the station. "Do you think there's anyone here?"

"Let's see."

The wind picked up as they crossed the yard, blowing cold, pelting them with grit and lifting dirt devils that beat against their backs and legs. Laurie shielded her face as Boon retrieved the saddlebags and took his Colt Lightning from the rifle sheath. Then he clasped her hand and ran with her across the dusty yard, past the well, ringed by crudely made brick with bits of straw sticking out. A bucket sitting upon the rim, suspended from a rope and pulley, fell into the well as they passed. Boon headed for the reddish-orange hut speckled with large patches of missing plaster that exposed the stacked clay brick. There was no window, just a scarred wooden door with so many nicks and chinks upon the surface that it looked as if it had been used for some sort of knife-throwing contest. There was a peek hole, closed and also shuttered, at about eye level.

She held down her skirt with both hands as Boon tried the door and found it barred.

He kicked with his boot heel. "Open up."

"Tarnation!" came a shout from inside. "Who's there?"

The peek hole flapped open, but Laurie could see no one there.

"You the stationmaster?" asked Boon.

"No, I'm the gal-dern president of Mexico. What do you think?"

"This here is Laurie Bender, daughter of Captain John Bender of the Texas Rangers."

The business end of the rifle emerged from the slot in the door, directed at Boon.

"And you are?"

He didn't answer that directly. "I'm bringing her back to her father. We was to meet here. He should have arrived already."

"Well, he ain't. Nor have I received any word on the last stage to expect him, so you two are trespassing. Only ones allowed here are those traveling with C. Bain & Company and the U.S. mail. So water your horses and skedaddle."

"But the storm," said Laurie.

"Wait it out in the stable if you like."

She and Boon exchanged a look.

"We need horses," he said.

The door flung open as a lightning flash preceded the boom of thunder.

"Changed my mind. Come inside."

Laurie glanced at Boon, who nodded, so she scooted in before him.

Boon followed her, closing the door against the blowing sand.

Laurie rubbed her eyes, succeeding only in working the grit farther in.

The interior was so dark that it took a moment for her eyes to adjust to the gloom, but she located the stationmaster. A scruffy, disheveled man stood clutching his rifle to his cheek.

Boon bolted the door then turned.

"Can't have you stealing my mules. They're good for nothing, but they're all I got."

"I'll trade our horses. Two three-year-old quarter horses and a scrappy mustang. Sound, but spent."

The stationmaster lifted a brow at that and lowered the barrel of the rifle.

"Why you in such a hurry? You just said yourself a storm's coming. Looks like a whopper, too."

The stationmaster resumed his seat, set the rifle beside him like an honored guest and lifted a forkful of beans to his mouth. He was not a neat eater, Laurie saw. She glanced away, surveying the low roof and exposed beams. Beside her lay a bench with a battered tin basin of dirty water and a cake of soap that seemed to have been rolled on the dirt floor judging from the flecks of grime that dotted it. The nail above the basin held a length of string long enough to allow a guest to use the comb attached to the other end, as if she would.

"We got company behind us," said Boon. "George Hammer and his men. We need the cover of the station or we got no chance."

"George..." This news rendered him speechless. His jaw clacked up and down a few times as his face turned scarlet. He rose to his feet so fast he upended the bench, sending his rifle tumbling over. He drew his arms through his sagging suspenders as he grabbed the gun. Then he hustled across the room, pausing to retrieve his hat and rubber slicker from the peg beside the door.

"Damn you both for bringing him to my door."

"You're leaving?" asked Laurie, but the answer was obvious, as his hand was already on the latch.

"The Apache robbed this station last year. Killed the last stationmaster. Would have got me, too, but I made it out the kitchen window after dark and hid in them cliffs out back."

"I could use another man," said Boon.

The man snorted. "And I could use a fast horse instead of a mean, pig-eyed mule. But you're crazy if you think I'm waiting for the Hammer to come a-knocking. You two have any sense, you best run on those spent horses. That'd be your only chance."

"But my father—"

"Will find you both dead." With that he threw open the door. The wind blew it open so that it crashed against the outside wall, sending more plaster to the ground. The yard had taken on the strange green color of an imminent storm as the wind howled like a living thing. Lightning flashed purple, blinding Laurie for a moment. Before she could even blink, the thunder crashed.

The stationmaster charged toward the stables, heedless of the weather, but his hat blew off and he lit off chasing it. Then he staggered as if pushed from behind. Laurie shielded her eyes to watch him, for he no longer ran but straightened, standing motionless for a moment. Then he dropped his slicker.

"What's the matter with him?" she called, trying to be heard above the whistling wind.

The man fell to his knees and Laurie now saw a crimson stain welling through the pale mustard-yellow flannel.

"Shot!" called Boon, shoving her backward so hard she fell to her backside as the top of the door frame exploded into chunks.

Wood splinters showered the floor as Boon slammed the door closed and lifted the beam into the metal holder, barring the entrance.

"Hammer!" called Boon.

Laurie wasn't sure if she heard gunfire or rain lashing against the walls.

"Stay down," Boon called as he went to the door, threw back the small latch and opened the peek hole, staying low as he slid the barrel of his rifle out the window. "There's nine riders in the yard." He squeezed off a quick shot. "Eight."

He ducked down as bullets whizzed through the opening and thudded into the wall opposite.

Boon rose again, firing in a rapid series of shots as Laurie crawled toward him.

"Seven. They're making for the stables. Six."

His rifle clicked, indicating he had emptied his weapon. Laurie scrambled to find ammunition and located two boxes on the shelf next to the flour. She brought them, but they were the wrong caliber.

Boon gave her a look. "Still got Freet's pistol?"

"Yes."

"You any good?"

"I can kill a stewed tomato can from forty paces."

"Good enough," he said.

Beyond the door, gunfire sounded, sharp beyond the hum of rain beating on the roof. He set aside the rifle and drew his pistol. Aiming it out the small flap door, he fanned the hammer like a gunfighter.

"I can reload for you," she said. "Where are your extra cartridges?"

He rummaged in his vest pocket and retrieved two rounds. "These for the rifle," he said, passing them to her with the gun. "All I got left are on my belt," said Boon, now flattened against the wall as he reloaded his revolver from the dwindling supply of bullets on his gun belt.

Laurie quickly slid the bullets into the rifle and held it ready.

The pistol replenished, Boon peered out the flap again. He fired once out the window.

"They've taken cover."

Laurie's eyes widened at that. "What shall we do?"

"I figure maybe they'll try to sneak around back while they draw fire from the front. When I'm out of ammo, they'll come through the roof or wait out the rain and burn us out. We have to make a run for it now or we'll be trapped in here."

"Where?"

"Out the kitchen window like the stationmaster said, and up those cliffs."

"They'll see us."

"The rain might cover us same as darkness. But we got little choice. They'll be around back soon. Best be gone before they take down that door or come through the roof."

"Without horses?"

He stared at her. "Maybe I can circle round to the stables and steal those mules."

"No." She was certain that was suicide. "We stay together and wait for my father."

Boon's face was grim.

"You don't think he's coming."

He drew a long breath and then stroked her cheek with his gloved hand. "If you were mine, I'd be here unless I was dead. Something happened. Something bad. Guess we're on our own."

His answer sent a chill down her spine.

He set the pistol to half cock and opened the loading lever. The cylinder dropped into his palm. He handed it over with a fistful of bullets. Laurie had never loaded a Remington, but she slid the bullets into place and handed it back. Boon snapped the lever into place.

Laurie held out Freet's gun to Boon.

"Four shots," she said.

He nodded and tucked the weapon in the front of his holster, beneath his belt buckle.

"We'll make for the cliffs, but if they come for us, if I'm not alive to protect you, Laurie, you got to use my mother's gun."

Laurie retrieved the little pistol from her skirt pocket, gripping it in her open hands as a cold sweat broke out all over her body.

"You understand? Don't let them take you alive."

She wrapped her icy fingers around the smooth hardwood grip and pressed the weapon to her bosom. Icy certainty settled in her heart. She would *not* be taken alive.

She met his troubled stare. “I understand.”

Chapter Fourteen

Laurie retrieved Boon's oilskin slicker and put it on as he instructed, then tucked the derringer into the pocket sewn into the side seam. The pistol thumped against her leg, reminding her of her final means of escape.

Boon had placed Freet's pistol in his empty holster and now clasped Laurie by the elbow and they dashed to the small window above a dingy table. Boon carried his empty rifle. He hesitated at the shuttered window.

"If they've surrounded us, we're finished," he said.

"And if we stay here?"

"Might last until the Rangers come."

She leveled a steady gaze upon him and shook her head.

He nodded. "Only chance is to get into those rocks and hide."

Laurie opened the shutter. Boon peered out into a gray curtain of rain so heavy he could just make out the hill some fifteen feet beyond. Someone pounded on the front door.

"Boon! Open up!"

"Cal, Hammer's second," he said and fired two shots through the center of the door. The third time he pulled the trigger, his rifle clicked uselessly. Boon laid aside the gun. "Can't waste any more bullets on him." He sounded remorseful at this. He looked down at Laurie and nodded, his decision made. "Let's go."

Boon jumped up on the table and then lifted Laurie up and out into the torrent. She landed in an ankle-deep lake that formed against the back wall. The rain pelted down, stinging her face, soaking her hair and sliding down the collar of the overlarge slicker. It was a deluge, a Biblical flood falling from above, sending newborn streams running all about her. Puddles splashed with the new raindrops. Laurie used one hand as a visor, searching for the outlaws, but seeing no one, while the other hand clutched the smooth grip of the derringer.

Two shots. Only two.

She turned to see Boon following her. He clasped her hand and they ran, blindly, splashing through the downpour. They stumbled up the incline that rose before them, dodging around rocks and past prickly pears, saw grass and muddy water pouring down from above in rivers. Scaling the white gypsum bluffs hand over hand, Laurie's skirts became a tangle, but he pushed from behind and shoved her up before him.

Behind them came the sound of gunfire, or was it just the pounding rain?

Laurie's sodden skirts weighed her down and the slicker flapped against her, impeding her steps, making her stagger. Boon righted her again. She was slowing them. And so she did an unladylike thing, lifting her skirts and the slicker all the way up to her waist, baring her legs to the cold stinging rain, and ran like an antelope up the steep incline. Boon stayed behind her, helping her, shielding her. The upward slope ceased so abruptly she fell onto the bluff above the stage station.

"We're on the top," she called, trying to be heard above the beating rain.

"Keep going."

Laurie looked back and noticed men behind them, dark outlines scrambling up the trail.

Boon saw her panicked expression and turned, firing three rounds from his pistol. The men dropped to the ground. An instant later, return fire sounded above the torrent.

The Hammer had found them.

Boon grabbed her hand and dragged her along, running with her to the nearest cover, then pushing her behind a clump of rock that jutted from the top of the butte. The men closed the distance between them by half.

How had they noticed their escape so fast?

Boon fired again. Laurie's brain clicked off the tally. Two shots left.

Laurie drew the other pistol from Boon's holster and took aim, waiting for a man to appear.

"Reload," she ordered.

She watched them coming, three men spread wide, and aimed at the center man. The flash and kick shocked her, hurting her wrist, and she nearly dropped the weapon. Her target staggered and fell.

"Oh," she cried, feeling the pain in her own chest as she realized what she had done. Had she killed him?

Boon had his pistol reloaded and took aim beside her.

The outlaws scrambled for cover, firing from behind rocks.

Boon fired all six shots. He removed his cartridge belt and handed it over, accepting the pistol he had given her and using it to hold them back as she reloaded. It was a tactic that could not last long.

"This is the last," she said. "Three rounds."

Boon accepted the pistol and they waited as the shots pinged off the stone above them. Boon peered around the rock.

"They're coming." He fired all three shots then ducked for cover again. "I think I got Cal."

Laurie offered the derringer.

He pushed it back toward her. "You keep it."

Their eyes met and held. He didn't have to remind her of what to do with that last shot.

Laurie drew the pistol against her frantically beating heart.

"I'm so sorry, Laurie. I'm sorry I couldn't save you."

"You did. You kept them from hurting me. I'll never forget that."

She reached for him and he took her up in his arms as their mouths met. The kiss was swift and full of the longing for what they would never have. Boon drew back, pushing her behind him.

The rain no longer swept in dark curtains, the storm now racing past them. The sky brightened as the rain continued to fall, gently, as if in apology.

She could hear the outlaws shouting back and forth.

Gunshots sounded again, but none pinged off the rocks before them. Her ears must have been playing tricks because the gunfire sounded as if it came from farther down the bluff.

Laurie peeked over the rock outcropping to see George Hammer running toward them, a knife in one hand and a pistol in the other. He was looking back over his shoulder instead of at them, and that was why he did not see Boon launch himself at Hammer. Laurie noticed three other outlaws charging at them. They did not stop to help their leader, but dashed past them, disappearing in the maze of irregular rock formations. What in the world?

More gunfire sounded.

Another man appeared, coming at a lope, rifle held at chest level. Laurie leveled the pistol but paused when she saw his rifle aimed at the retreating band of outlaws. Laurie glanced at Boon, still fighting Hammer. He was ten feet off and the outlaw's pistol lay beside them. They now rolled and tumbled back and forth as each tried to stab the other with the knife they both gripped.

Another man appeared at the mesa bluff and Laurie swung the pistol back in that direction. Two shots, she remembered, one for Hammer, one for her. She had none left for whatever was coming up the hill.

George Hammer rolled to straddle Boon. Hammer used his head as a battering ram against Boon's forehead. Hammer took possession of the knife and raised it. Laurie took aim and squeezed the trigger.

A piece of Hammer's hat tore as the bullet whizzed by. Hammer glanced in her direction. In that instant Boon cocked a fist and landed a blow to the outlaw's jaw. Hammer fell backward, but quickly scrambled for his pistol and swung it in Boon's direction. He raised the weapon and Laurie did not hesitate. She closed one eye, sighted the center of Hammer's chest and squeezed the trigger.

Two shots sounded simultaneously, one from a rifle behind her and one from the empty derringer Laurie held in her trembling hand.

George Hammer arched, dropping his knife.

He stared at her as he lifted both arms in surrender. He stood, took two staggering steps in her direction when another rifle shot popped from behind her and he fell back into the mud, staring openmouthed at the cloudy sky, heedless of the rain. Boon staggered to his feet.

Someone shouted, “Go after the others.”

Laurie recognized the voice.

She turned and saw the shooter lowering his rifle, the dull gleam of the Texas star pinned to the man’s hat. Her heart pounded in her throat as the first glimmer of hope burst upon her like a beam of sunlight from the heavens.

Laurie looked at the man beside the shooter as he motioned behind him. He turned and pointed with his Colt revolver in the direction the outlaws had taken. Taller than the rifleman, he wore his star pinned to his slicker. He turned to her and she met cold blue eyes, so different from her own, but almost as familiar.

“Papa!” she cried, crawling to her feet.

The rifleman lifted his head at her cry, revealing gray eyes and a bushy black mustache, and Laurie recognized him, also. This was Sam Coats, her father’s second in command and the best shot among them. She should have known it was him, for the two were inseparable.

The second shot, which she had heard as she fired Boon's mother's pistol, had come from his gun. She closed her eyes and prayed that it was his bullet, and not hers, that had killed Hammer, for despicable as the outlaw may have been, she feared another dark mark on her soul.

Coats set off at a lope after the fleeing outlaws, calling over his shoulder, "Come on, boys."

More of her father's men appeared from cover, taking off after Coats.

John Bender walked slowly toward the Hammer's still body and fired two more bullets into his chest, directly over his heart. Laurie winced and covered her mouth to keep the cry from escaping her.

Hammer did not move. Her father holstered his weapon in the well-worn, finely tooled leather sheath and opened his arms to his daughter. But Laurie ran to Boon, throwing herself at him, wrapping her arms around him.

"Are you hurt?" she cried.

"No."

Laurie pulled back to see his sodden sleeve red with blood. It ran in watery rivulets down his hand and onto the knife he still held.

She turned to her father. “Oh, Papa, he’s bleeding!”

John Bender took hold of Laurie, pulling her away from Boon. Her impulse was to yank her arm free and latch on to Boon again, but she thought better of it and stood stiff and uncertain as her father turned his attention back to Boon.

“Can you walk, son?”

“Yes, sir.”

“Come on then.”

Boon clutched his arm and rose slowly to his feet. Laurie tried to go to Boon’s side, but her father restrained her, clasping her elbow a little too tightly. “He can make it.”

Her father held her as they retraced their steps to the trailhead, leaving Boon behind. Laurie stopped, forcing the captain to do so, as well. His mouth was a tight line as he lifted one brow in her direction.

“He’s hurt,” she whispered.

Two of his men reached them, taking her father’s attention away from her. Laurie felt she could breathe again and she craned her neck to see Boon making his way toward them, his face also grim, his fingers gripping his injured upper arm so tightly they were ghostly white. She felt a tug in his direction pulling deep in her belly. As if sensing her intention, her father's hold upon her forearm tightened.

"We got them all, Captain," said Murdock, a tall, thin Ranger whose mustache curled like a pig's tail on each side of his mouth, despite the rain.

"Bandage Boon and bring him down."

"Yes, sir," said Murdock, already reaching to untie his bandanna. She'd seen the large swathe of colorful cloth used for everything from a dust cover to a sling and thought it only slightly less vital than a man's rifle.

Her father turned her toward the stage station. On their descent the rain changed again, the drops small and infrequent. Still she shivered now, her blouse and skirts soaked down the front from the gap in the open slicker.

"I shot a man," she said.

"I saw. Broke his upper arm."

Laurie felt a moment's relief that she had not killed him.

"Coats finished him."

"I shot Hammer, too."

"No, that was Coats, as well."

Something about the way he said it made it seem certain, as if just by saying so, he could make it true. But she knew one of her bullets had struck Hammer, no matter what he said. As she considered it, the horror of shooting a man washed away against the grim certainty that George Hammer had deserved to die.

The yard had turned into a quagmire of red mud that clung to her hem. She walked with her head up and shoulders back trying to look brave as the daughter of a famous Ranger, trying to pretend she had survived untouched.

"Laurie, cover yourself." Her father lifted a finger to indicate her bosom.

The rain had soaked her bodice and it clung to her skin, revealing the swell of her breasts and the hard knots of her nipples. Laurie gasped and folded her arms across herself, hunching now in embarrassment as he hurried her past the bodies of the outlaws who had come to kill Boon and capture her.

Two of her father's men stood over one corpse, discussing the bullet wound in the outlaw's cheek. Laurie's blood now felt as cold as her skin. She stumbled along, humiliated, ashamed and weakened. Rescue had come, but instead of elation she felt only misery.

Her father guided her into the adobe hut and ordered one of his men to bring a blanket for her to cover herself. Laurie removed Boon's slicker and dutifully wrapped the coarse green wool about herself, veiling herself from neck to knee. Her feet squished inside her shoes but her father indicated that she dare not remove them as she sat before the smoldering fire.

"Wait here," he said before ducking back into the rain.

Laurie waited in the dirty hut, listening to the rain patter. She glanced toward the window where she and Boon made their desperate escape. If only they could have kept running.

The world had caught her at last. She was back in her father's keeping and her stomach roiled with worry as she rocked slowly back and forth, eyes set on the packed earthen floor.

Where was Boon? Was he all right?

After many minutes passed she began to stare hopefully at the door. She recalled the blood on Boon's shirt, and rose. Then remembered her father's orders to stay and folded back to her place, staring at the door.

Her father's partner, Sam Coats, came in, nodding as he removed his hat. The brim and crown were soaked, turning the tan hat brown, but the area above the hatband had remained dry. The fine braid had been made from the tail hairs of Sam Coats's favorite horse, killed in action against Mexican rustlers some years ago, according to her father.

"Glad to see you well, Miss Laurie. Your pa was beside himself."

"Was he?" She saw no indication of any emotion except annoyance.

"Would have been here sooner but we ran into Apache raiders."

"Is everyone all right?"

Coats nodded. "We chased them a-ways, but had to turn back."

Now *his* look held annoyance, as if she had spoiled their fun.

"Where is Boon?"

"They got him in the stable."

"Tending him?"

Coats made a gesture that was decidedly noncommittal.

Laurie rose.

Coats motioned back to the bench. "Your pa asked me to stay with you."

Laurie felt dizzy at what she was about to do. She had always done as she was told and had never disobeyed her father before. She knew Boon's wounds needed tending. Laurie stiffened her spine.

"I'm going out."

"No, Miss Laurie. Stay put."

"Then you bring Boon in."

Coats shook his head. "I follow orders, same as you."

Laurie took a tentative step. Would he bar the door, grab her, force her back to her seat? She took another step.

"Laurie, he's already vexed at you for leaving the station with a complete stranger."

That had been stupid. She had kicked herself all the way to the outlaws' camp over that blunder. All Rangers wore their badge on their hat or their lapel when on business, not secreted in their pockets. But by the time she knew she was in danger, it had been too late. Laurie reached the door and opened it. Steam rose from the ground, but the rain had ceased. She held the blanket like a mantle and left the station. Coats caught up with her, walking at her side.

"Best turn around."

"I am not your daughter, Mr. Coats. I do not take orders from you."

The mud sucked at her shoes.

Coats blocked her advance. "I'm your father's representative."

"You'll excuse me if I follow my own mind in this matter. Now stand aside, Mr. Coats."

Chapter Fifteen

Bender stood with one boot resting on a dusty wooden crate, well inside the stable, regarded by two gray mules with long ears and bristly chins, while Boon sat on a low bench against their stall. The rest of his men waited outside.

Boon faced Laurie's father alone.

"The Rangers will pick up any medical bill resulting from this injury. I'll also clear you of any charges. You've earned a fresh start, son. Reckon you could ride shotgun again or try riding herd somewheres."

Boon understood the implication. His job was finished. The captain had no further use for him and was sending him off to get him away from Laurie. He'd cleared his name, more than he deserved. Still it irked him to have the proof that he'd been used.

Bender didn't want him near his men and certainly not near his little girl.

"I reckon it will," he said, trying not to show this man the depth of his pain. This man for whom he was willing to give everything had thrown him away just like everyone else he ever cared about.

But despite what the captain wanted, Boon still had an obligation, not to Bender, but to his daughter. Laurie, once the means to ingratiate himself to this Ranger, was now much, much more.

He had brought her home, but not safe. Boon had bedded her and so he would be staying around until he was certain she did not need him.

"Might stay awhile, though," he said, trying to make his decision sound casual.

"Why's that?"

Boon shrugged. "Make sure Laurie's all right."

Bender leaned in, forearm on his knee, opposite hand on his hip. The smile still fixed on his lips, but his cold eyes narrowing, hardening. "She's my daughter, son. That makes her welfare *my* responsibility."

Should he tell him what had happened or wait it out? He didn't want to spoil Laurie's chances of marrying that damned banker, even though the thought of it stuck in his throat like a fish bone.

Boon shrugged again. "Might like to work for you again."

Bender straightened, glancing away and then back. "Well, I don't have any openings at present. But if you would like, I expect I could find something for you down in McAllen. Got friends ranching there."

Yes, that was a good long way from Fort Worth and Laurie.

The generous offer showed just how much Bender wanted him gone from here. The captain was sending him off. Boon knew why. Laurie had revealed her feelings for him when she'd seen his arm wound. Running to him, holding him. Her father was no fool. Boon was not the sort he wanted near his girl, not the sort *anyone* wanted near their girl. The funny thing was that he agreed with Bender, and if he could, he'd leave right now.

But he couldn't.

He'd not leave Laurie, frightened, alone and without means. He'd not leave her to face what the girls at the Blue Belle had faced, shunned, shamed and desperate. He couldn't change what he had done, but he could protect her from that.

"There some particular reason you need to see that Laurie is all right, son?"

Boon brought his attention back to Captain John Bender. He should have known. Men like this Ranger went at a problem headfirst.

Boon nodded. "Yes, sir. There is."

Bender's pistol was out before Boon could lift his hands in surrender.

"You bedded her? My little girl?"

Boon looked down the barrel of the captain's pistol and nodded. "Yes, sir."

Bender cocked his pistol. "You son of a bitch. I oughta shoot you where you stand."

He said nothing because he felt much the same. He had as much right to Laurie as a flea had to a dog.

"Yes, sir" was all he could think to say.

"Did anyone else touch her?"

"Just me."

"I sent you in there to protect her."

And Boon knew he had failed. But he wouldn't fail her again. And he'd be damned if he'd apologize to the captain for taking the best thing that ever came his way. Bender could shoot him if he wanted, otherwise he was staying.

"Maybe so, but I ain't taking a job in McAllen. I'm staying 'til I know she's all right."

Bender spun his gun across and struck Boon a mighty blow to his temple. He saw a bright starburst of light and heard a shriek, like a steam engine whistle. Then he was falling slowly through space, but he never felt himself land.

Laurie stepped into the stable with Coats one pace back, in time to see her father strike Boon in the head with the butt end of his pistol. Boon's scalp split open and blood sprayed down his face as his eyes rolled back white.

Laurie screamed, a high piercing wail of pain and horror as she held her hands to her face, allowing the blanket to fall behind her on the ground.

Her father turned, looked past her to Coats. "I told you to keep her in the station."

"Wouldn't stay put," said his second, now grasping Laurie's elbow and tugging her out the door.

Laurie wrenched free and when Coats lunged, she slapped him hard across his face.

His eyes went wide. Laurie felt her scalp tingling as she realized what she had done. She stood frozen before him as her heart slammed against her ribs. Then she heard Boon moan and all else faded.

She ran to him, dropping to her knees, wrapping her arms around him and turning him to his back. Blood filled the socket of his eye and rolled into his ear.

"No, no, no," Laurie chanted as her brain threatened to shut down on her.

Her eyes fixed on Boon's kerchief and she tried to release the knot, but her fingers were shaking so badly she had to squeeze them into fists to steady them before trying again. So much blood and there was a lump as hard as a knot on a tree, there on Boon's head, just above his hairline. A jagged wound stretched across the knot, the ugly gash her father had given him.

She folded the cloth into a square and pressed it to the wound. In a moment her fingers were warm and sticky with his blood. She removed the neckerchief and folded it twice more before returning it to its place, pressing hard, praying hard.

She glanced to her father, wanting his help, knowing she would not get it. When their eyes met she saw the icy-blue glint of fury aimed like a pistol right at her.

There was no question in her mind. He knew exactly what she and Boon had done and he hated her for it.

"I thought you'd know better than to lift your skirts to the likes of him," he said, his tone low, murderous.

"He rescued me," she whispered.

"He raped you and I'll see him hanged."

She gasped, then shook her head, meeting the hatred in his eyes. "No, he didn't."

Her father turned his back on her. Laurie could not keep the tears from coming, choking her, blurring her sight and welling within her soul. It was hard to have her father look at her like this. The father she had always adored, the one for whom she had tried to be the perfect lady, now knew exactly the sort of woman she had become.

Laurie lowered her head in disgrace, frozen by the realization that he could see her now as she truly was. But despite the humiliation, she would not hide the truth at the cost of Boon's life.

Boon moaned and his eyes fluttered. She gazed down at him, knowing he had taken the blow that should have been hers.

"If it wasn't for him, I'd be dead," she whispered.

Her father squatted beside her. Did he think she would have been better off dead than to have come back to him in shame?

"Men got ways of taking what they want."

She could scarcely whisper the words. "But he didn't take me, Papa. I gave myself to him."

She could not look at him, could not bear to see the disappointment there in his cool blue eyes.

"He's an outlaw, Laurie. And he took advantage of you."

"He didn't."

"A rustler, a thief."

Laurie kept her chin tucked and her head down as she spoke. "Then why did you send him?"

"Only choice. I wanted you alive." His mustache twitched as he said it. "So I sent him."

So Boon was right, Laurie realized. Her father had used him.

"Then he did as you asked." She looked down at Boon's bloody face. "And this is his reward."

She stared up at her father, wondering if she knew him at all.

Her father growled and stood up, calling to

Coats. "Call two men to carry him into the station." Then he turned to Laurie. "You best hope you are not with child."

Her father walked away.

Laurie sat beside Boon with her mouth open, one hand holding the cloth to his cheek, wondering why the possibility of a baby no longer filled her with horror, but with a tiny twinkle of hope. She knew what Boon was. She also knew that her father could not have done better. Boon was impressed into the outlaws' gang the same way she was impressed into a situation with Anton. It wasn't his fault. She lifted her head. And it wasn't her fault, either.

She understood that now. And this time, with Boon, was different because she had wanted it. So she'd take the consequences, whatever they were. Having a baby, Boon's baby, would not be a shame, at least not to her.

It might be the first good thing to happen to her in years.

Convincing her parents of that would be another matter. Laurie placed one hand upon her belly and gathered herself for the approaching storms.

Chapter Sixteen

Laurie knew there was something wrong with Boon when he didn't rouse even when she bathed his face with cold water. The Rangers found an old blue Studebaker wagon in the stable and loaded Boon in the back.

She elected to ride in the box of the wagon, behind the driver, mules and entire escort of Texas Rangers. Her father left three Rangers behind to bury the dead and one to wire Valencia about her daughter's safe return.

The old stage road was relatively good and they made thirty miles an hour, but by sundown they were less than half the distance to San Antonio. The Rangers made camp. Laurie stayed with Boon in the wagon, coaxing him awake enough to drink some black coffee.

She checked his wounded arm, seeing that the Rangers had only bandaged his injury with a dirty neckerchief. Had they heard nothing of Pasteur's germ theory? At the very least, his wound merited cleaning with soap and water. She washed him, seeing that the neat slice of Hammer's blade had cut a four-inch gash along his arm. The edges now looked pink and the muscle below had been exposed. She'd bandaged him with the clean cloth, laid a cold compress on his forehead and waved off the flies that tried to land on the cut upon his cheek.

She felt like herself again, before girls' school and lessons on deportment. She was useful again and capable. She drew in a long breath and let it go. There was something to be said about being who you are.

Her father prepared her a bedroll, which she accepted but abandoned when the men were asleep, to return to Boon.

Her father had hit him hard, too hard. Laurie understood that violence was a part of her father. His rougher side was what made him good at his job, but seeing the results of her father's brutality made her wonder if he was any better than Boon. Perhaps the difference between them wasn't so great after all, only the difference of a peso star.

Why wouldn't Boon wake? She brushed her fingers over his brow and Boon stared up at her.

"Boon?" Something about his eyes didn't look quite right. "Are you awake?"

He looked at her with a serious expression, his eyes glassy.

"Are you sad, Laurie? Even after I brung you home to them? Are you still sad?"

The tears began to flow. She did not trust her voice, so she nodded in a jerking motion as her chin trembled in her effort to hold back the weeping.

"Why you still sad, Laurie-gal?" His hand reached for her but he couldn't keep it steady and he missed her cheek by several inches.

She captured his hand and wove her fingers through his, bringing them to her damp face and kissing his knuckles. And that was when she felt the unnatural heat of his skin, the dry, frightening heat of fever. She gasped as she stared down at him.

"Don't be afraid. I won't let them take you," he whispered, looking up at her.

Was he still back there, riding for their lives? She closed her eyes wishing she could return to their waterfall, safe and hidden from the real world.

"We're safe, Boon," she whispered, stroking one hand over his forehead as she held his other hand to her cheek.

His voice was hushed and his eyes wide. "Safe?"

"Yes. We're going home."

He grinned as if she had said something funny. "Ah, Laurie, I don't have a home."

She felt a stab of remorse for him and all he had not had and then wondered if her parents might put her out. It wasn't unheard-of, to renounce a wayward wife or daughter. What would become of her then?

"Oh, Boon. I am so frightened."

He stared up at her. "I'll protect you, Laurie. I'll always protect you."

His eyes fluttered shut and she could not rouse him again. She unbuttoned his shirt and used the cloth to bathe his chest, neck and face. She worked through the night, catching herself dozing sitting up beside him.

"Laurie?"

She startled awake, glancing down at Boon, but he still slept his feverish, restless slumber. She looked around to see her father standing beside the buckboard.

"What are you doing here?"

She rubbed the sleep from her eyes and scrubbed her face with the palms of her hands before facing him again.

"Boon has a fever."

"I'll send someone to tend him."

She didn't argue, but neither did she leave him as the camp broke with the dawn. Laurie bathed him until they reached San Antonio, at which time her father insisted she sit properly in the wagon box beside Murdock.

As soon as they were within the town limits her father directed them to a home, one of its shingles pronouncing a Dr. Archie P. Langor in residence.

Boon was carried into one of the treatment rooms.

Laurie tried to follow but her father blocked her entrance, pointing to a bench in the reception room.

"Wait there," he ordered, and shut the door in her face.

Laurie stood staring at the door weighing her options. Finally she did as he bid her. After a silent eternity, her father and the doctor emerged, blocking her view of the room beyond.

Dr. Langor wiped his hands on a clean towel

and then threw it over his left shoulder like a waiter.

"Stitched him up with silk thread. Going to have to watch for infection for a day or two. He is far from out of the woods. The boy has lost a lot of blood and his fever is still high."

"Who will look after him?" Laurie asked.

"Not you," said her father.

Dr. Langor intervened. "Does he have family?"

"No," said Laurie.

"Then I'll put him up in a boardinghouse where he can get care."

"He can come with us. I will see to him."

"No," declared her father. "You'll not be caring for that young buck anymore." His father turned his back on her, facing the doctor now. "You send me the bill, Doc. Glad to pay it."

She stood, wringing her hands. She knew she should stay silent. But her reputation suddenly seemed less important than Boon's welfare.

"He brought me to safety and we are not foisting him on strangers." She had no idea where she found the courage to say any of it, but she stood there on shaky ground as her father blinked in astonishment. He looked as if he did not recognize his own daughter. "Papa, Boon saved my life. We owe him a debt of gratitude."

Her father glanced at the doctor and then lowered his chin and glared, telling her without words that he wasn't happy about airing dirty laundry in public. "Let me be clear. The doc here gets that boy back on his feet and back in the saddle. Then he rides away."

Laurie swallowed hard. Boon understood, even back then, that her father had no intention of keeping him as one of his men and that his yearning to be a Ranger was just a pipe dream. Why hadn't she?

Laurie simmered like a teakettle about to boil. It wasn't fair. Boon was a good man who had made a hard choice to stay alive. While Anton was a bad man who had made the easy choice and become a Ranger. Laurie glared at her father, knowing that if she fought him now, Boon would receive no further care.

"Laurie?" There was menace in her father's voice.

Laurie crumbled like week-old bread. She folded her hands and nodded. "Yes, Papa."

"That's my girl." He patted her arm.

Why did she feel like a mouse scampering for cover?

"Dr. Langor?" she asked. "Is there anything wrong with his mind, from the blow to the head, I mean?"

"Can't tell yet." He lifted his fingers and ticked off a list. "Bleeding, wound, fever and then we'll see about the rest."

Her father thanked the doctor and escorted Laurie out, making their way, on foot, to a hotel near the rail depot, where he rented a suite of rooms.

"Nobody knows you were captured. Your mother wired me when she discovered you left and I got you back safe, if not sound." He stared at her middle pointedly. "So you keep quiet about where you been. That's what your mother would advise, I'm certain. She's big on a woman's reputation. Seems that didn't rub off on you."

Laurie forced her shoulders back and continued to walk, even though she felt as fragile as a dried leaf.

"I'll wire your ma that I'll be putting you on a train tomorrow."

It seemed he could not be rid of her fast enough. But Laurie was no longer the girl he remembered or the woman she had sought to become. Despite her mother's lessons on etiquette, her ordeal had only served to illuminate, to her at least, that she was more like her father than either of them could have imagined.

Laurie paused in the thoroughfare to face him and her father drew to a halt beside her, the disapproval plain on his face.

"No," she said.

"No?"

"I will not be boarding a train. I will remain here until I am certain Boon is well and that he will not be harmed."

"How you aim to do that, exactly?"

"Well, if you do not assist me, I suppose I could find someone who would, a newspaper man perhaps."

Her father snatched up her elbow and dragged her along with him. "I do not respond well to threats, little lady. And you do not rule this roost."

Laurie said nothing, though she was not through yet. She was hustled down a wooden walkway beside the manure-strewn road toward the hotel where her father had lived since his departure from their home.

"Your mother said you boarded that train without her say. That true?"

She nodded.

"We didn't even know you was missing.

Damn foolish thing to do. Whatever possessed you?"

"I came to tell you that Mother has a suitor. He's asked her to marry him and she is considering his proposal."

"What?" he bellowed, his face turning purple. Clearly he did not like this news any better than Laurie had. "She's my wife!"

"Not since the judge granted the divorce decree."

"A piece of paper don't change what is between us."

Her father was still shaking his head when they entered the lobby. The clerk behind the desk shot out to offer him a telegram. Bender stopped to read it and frowned.

"Your mother's coming today, with Paloma." He glanced at the clock mounted on the wall. "Damnation, train's already arrived." Her father removed his hat, finger combed his hair, and then straightened his bolo as if preparing to meet her that instant. He reached in his pocket and handed off his key. "Go up and wait, just in case I miss her. Lord, that woman can still make me jump like a bullfrog on a string."

Laurie considered going to Dr. Langor's office, but she was dirty and tired and wanted to wash up, so she dragged herself up the stairs and had not even time to wash her face when a knock sounded at the door.

From the hallway, her mother called her name.

Laurie fairly flung the door off its hinges.

There before her stood Valencia Sanchez Garcia, exactly as Laurie had last seen her mother: petite, with black hair that Laurie had inherited along with her small, curvy figure and dark eyes. Her mother was not Mexican, but Castilian, from a good family who were not pleased about her attraction to a wild Texan.

Valencia gave a cry that might have been joy or horror and then embraced her daughter, tears streaming copiously down her cheeks.

Laurie's mother kissed her and hugged her, as she enfolded her against her small, warm body. Laurie clung, finding herself also reduced to tears. Her mother drew back to look at her.

Paloma directed the porter and then showed him out. With the click of the door, her mother spoke.

"Didn't he even think to order you a bath? Where is he? I will tear him apart."

"Mama, we only just arrived, not an hour ago. He's gone to meet you at the train."

Her mother's mouth still pulled down at the corners. She tightened her lips. "He left you to meet me? Oh, that man! How could he leave you alone?"

Laurie had the impression that he was anxious to meet his wife, but she kept silent.

Valencia separated from Laurie. "*Mi hija,* just look at you. But you're safe now and everything will be all right." Her mother drew back and faced Paloma.

Paloma was the color of gingerbread, tough as hardwood and straight and thin as a reed. Only the deep lines in her face and threads of silver in her dark hair betrayed her age. She had hands thick and tough from working but Valencia saw that her clothing was better than average quality, neat and well made, because a servant is a reflection of the master, or so her mother said.

Her mother spoke in Spanish. "Paloma, a bath for Laura, if you please."

Paloma nodded and left them alone.

Valencia turned back to her daughter. "They didn't hurt you? I couldn't bear it if they hurt you."

Laurie shut her eyes and shook her head. "Boon saved me."

Her mother pulled back. "Who?"

"Boon."

"Is that one of your father's new men?"

Laurie shook her head. Her mother clasped Laurie's face between her two hands and stared hard. Then Valencia swept her daughter into the room and seated them on a sofa as if this were her hotel room.

"Tell me everything."

Laurie was no longer a child and she knew better than to tell her mother everything. She certainly would keep some of what happened between her and Boon private. The trouble was, her mother was very keen and did not miss much. Even if she didn't say, her mother might still make assumptions.

Laurie drew a long breath and then began the telling. They sat side by side on the sofa, Laurie in her ruined purple skirts and stained blouse and her mother dressed in a fine moss-colored chambray day dress that accentuated her pale skin.

If her mother noted the places where she stumbled or the gaps where she withheld what she and Boon had done together, she did not comment, but her sharp eyes seemed to take in everything. When Laurie had talked herself out, her mother said, "I think I need to meet this boy."

"Papa won't let me see him."

"Well, thankfully, I no longer fall under your father's jurisdiction and so I do as I please. But you, *mi hija,* have to protect your reputation. Does anyone know where you have been?"

"I don't know. The doctor maybe."

"Well, your father dragged you through town looking like this." She swept a slim, elegant hand before Laurie. "Anyone with eyes will speculate. I shall have to have a reason for your condition. Perhaps a horse threw you and you rolled down a hill." Her mother considered her as if she were a problem to be solved. "Have you lost your bustle?"

Laurie's shoulders rounded, knowing the questioning had only just begun. The exhaustion of the journey, the escape, the attack and the night spent nursing Boon seemed to press upon her. Still, she needed to say aloud what plagued her most, the feeling that would not leave her. It hovered like a hummingbird over a blossom. Dared she say it aloud?

"Mama, I think I may have feelings for him."

Her mother sighed and then shook her head slowly as if Laurie had just spoken nonsense. In her dark eyes Laurie saw indulgence and sadness. "You only think that because you were afraid and he was there to help you. But he was there because your father sent him. It is natural for a drowning girl to cling to anything that is sent in her direction. But this is not love, it is dependence. You don't need him now…so the feeling will fade."

Laurie listened to this very rational explanation of her jumbled emotions. Could her mother be right?

"But I think—"

Her mother lifted a hand to stop her. "It is not possible, Laura."

Laurie stopped speaking, recognizing the sharp note in her mother's voice signaled the end of this discussion. To continue would lead nowhere.

Her mother smiled and stroked her hair. "When have you last slept?"

"I don't know."

A large copper tub was delivered along with a screen and a bucket brigade of maids carrying hot water. Paloma was efficient at getting things done.

Her mother directed them to set up the bath

in her father's bedchamber, commandeering the territory more smoothly than any invading army.

"Here, let's get you washed."

Laurie retreated behind the screen. She had removed her skirt and was unfastening her blouse when her mother returned. Laurie hesitated.

"Well?" said her mother.

Laurie slowly removed her blouse. She slipped her arms from the sleeves and let the blouse fall. Her soiled skirt followed until she stood in only the dirty chemise, torn stockings and black boots.

"Bustle, corset, bloomers, new stockings and garters, half crinoline and two petticoats." Her mother finished her survey of Laurie's attire and met her eyes again. "And hairpins, ribbons and a straw hat."

Laurie's eyes welled.

"Is that all?" she asked.

Laurie nodded.

"I've brought your things. You get washed up and I'll lay them out."

Her mother left Laurie behind the screen, so she quickly dragged off the filthy chemise and tossed it aside, stepping into the water.

She sank into the copper tub with a sigh

then scrubbed away the sand and dirt, feeling the sting of soap and water against the many small scrapes and scratches she had suffered during her ordeal. But her wounds were minor compared to Boon's.

She washed her hair twice, standing to rinse herself once more with clean water before wrapping up in an absorbent white linen cloth towel.

Her mother had laid out Laurie's nightgown and folded back the covers of her father's bed.

"Paloma will brush your hair and then you are going to bed. I will be right in the next room. When you wake, I will order supper."

She donned the clean chemise that Paloma handed her.

Were it not for the twinges in her muscles as she lifted her arms into the sleeves and the aching in her heart, she might even succeed in pretending that nothing had happened.

But she had tried that once before. Hiding her secret about Anton had only brought her shame and stolen her confidence. And Boon's words were true; Anton had taken advantage of her. Her crime had not been wickedness but gullibility.

Paloma motioned her to a seat and drew the

comb through Laurie's wet dark hair. When she tried to braid it, Laurie waved her off.

"I'll do it."

Paloma nodded, leaving the familiar white ribbon on the dressing stand. Her duty done, she left Laurie with an admonishment spoken in Spanish.

"You be good and do not worry your mama anymore or you make her sick."

Laurie watched the housekeeper exit to the hall directly and suddenly found herself alone for the first time since her departure. She stood and stared at herself in the large oval mirror beside her father's dressing table. Her reflection looked identical, but she was no longer the same on the inside. She felt like a stranger in her own skin. Even her snowy white nightdress felt strange.

But if she didn't belong here in her parents' care, where did she belong?

Laurie swept the hairbrush through her hair as the answer whispered through her. *You belong with him.*

Her mother said it was fear that drove her to Boon and perhaps that was so. But she was not frightened now. She was safe, she was home and she was miserable.

This was just an adjustment, she told herself. She'd been through a terrible ordeal; it was natural to feel anxious and sad.

Wasn't it?

The hairbrush slipped from her fingers as Laurie began to cry.

What was the matter with her?

Chapter Seventeen

Boon woke feeling as if someone had taken a wedge to his head and used it to split his skull in two. What had happened? He tried to lift his hands to cover his eyes, shield them from the light pouring in past his closed eyelids, and discovered that his left arm pained him, as well.

He tried to think back, but thinking was hard. His mind was fuzzy as the back of a sheep and felt just as dull and cottony. What could he recall?

Riding.

Riding hard with Laurie, her skirts flying, hair rolling out behind her like a curtain as they fled…

Where was Laurie?

The Hammer.

That brought Boon upright.

"Laurie!" He forced his eyes open. The light blinded him, increasing the pain, so he called out.

"Easy, son. Lie back now." Firm hands gripped his shoulders and pressed him back to the bedding.

"Laurie?" he asked.

"Safe, son. You brought her home safe."

Boon dropped into the pillows, his body urging him to slip back into the darkness, back into the cool, calm, but this time he fought it.

"Where is she?" he croaked, hardly recognizing his own voice.

"With her folks. You are in San Antonio. I am Dr. Langor and you had one mean gash across your head and another on your arm. Stitched it up with silk thread."

Boon made a tentative exploration of the knot on his head, feeling the scabs and puckering where the skin was stitched. The memories nibbled at him like a fish trying the bait. He'd fought Hammer. Someone had shot the outlaw.

Laurie.

Boon stilled at that memory. Laurie Bender, the proper daughter of the fiercest Ranger in Texas, had killed George Hammer, the meanest individual in the state. She was more like her father than she knew.

But there was a second shooter, a rifleman. Who was that?

Captain Bender's partner, the man who opted to hang Boon the minute they caught him, had saved his life.

Boon remembered returning to the station and one of the Rangers had given him his kerchief to stop the blood. Captain Bender had questioned him. He'd told her father the truth and… Boon closed his eyes, reliving the shock and then the dizziness. It hadn't even hurt really, but he'd been so surprised and then… had he blacked out?

"How'd I get here?"

"The Rangers brought you yesterday. Captain Bender requested he be summoned if you showed signs of rousing. I have sent for him. He seemed very keen to see you."

"Imagine so." Likely wanted to plant a bullet in him. Wouldn't blame the man if he did. Not after what he'd done with his daughter.

He longed to see Laurie again, just to hear her voice and know that she was all right. But she was with her family now. Of course she didn't need him. Unless that one night of lovemaking led her to motherhood. If she came through it all right, he'd give her what she wanted and leave her as he found her, not quite a virgin but at least she could be quit of him, while he'd never be quit of her.

Boon threw a hand over his throbbing eyes, knowing that he would leave Laurie when he was certain she didn't need him because that was what was best for her.

He'd go because he loved her.

He groaned.

"What time is it?"

"Early. You have been out since yesterday. I've got opiates, but I will hold off until I can better assess the condition of your brain."

It wasn't his brain that troubled him, but his heart. Laurie Bender had plumb stolen it right out from under his nose. He'd gone in to get her, trying to please her father, trying to prove he was tough enough to be a Ranger, and instead had discovered he wasn't tough at all. A little dark-haired girl had bested him, reeled him in and landed him. But she would throw him back soon enough, because ladies like Laurie Bender did not take up with outlaw sons of bitches like him.

He'd been alone all his life and never felt it like this before. Being alone was a damn sight different than giving up the one good thing that had ever come into your life.

"He still awake?"

That was the captain's voice. Boon stiffened and wiped his eyes. Damned if he'd let the captain see him cry.

"He was a minute ago."

"Give us the room, will you, Doc?"

"Certainly."

Boot heels clicked across hardwood floors. Boon uncovered his eyes and squinted, his stomach pitching like an unbroken horse under first saddle, but he swung his legs off the bed and, with the help of the head rail, pulled himself upright.

Once the door was closed behind them, Captain Bender leveled him with a steady look. Boon's head pounded and his hands were shaking. He needed to sit down, but he'd be damned if he would. He only hoped the captain would get on with it before he threw up or fell over.

It seemed a thousand years ago that he had stood before the Texas Ranger and been told that the captain had a mission just for him. *Bring her back home by any means necessary.* Well, Boon had done it, and in the process he had fallen in love with the captain's daughter.

"I come to offer you the reward money for Hammer," said Bender. "You earned it and it would give you a stake to get started someplace else."

The Ranger didn't mince words—he still wanted Boon gone, but now he tried honey instead of vinegar. The thought of being bought off stirred a fury in him, instantly settling his stomach and straightening his spine. Damned if he'd go on his say-so.

"Your daughter is the one who shot him," said Boon. "Give it to her."

"You're not to tell anyone that. She has enough to live down without word of that leaking out."

Boon nodded his acceptance of that.

"With or without the reward, best for you to leave town."

Boon couldn't move his head without the pain half blinding him.

"I'm here until I'm sure she won't need me."

"Well, she don't." Bender tucked his thumbs under the large silver buckle. "I'll find her a husband quick if I need to."

That news hit Boon harder than the barrel of Bender's pistol.

"I'm still staying 'til I know."

"You're going, just as soon as you can sit

a horse because staying is gonna prove real bad for your health. I've offered you the reward. I'll go a step further and offer you a job punching cows over in El Paso with a friend of mine. That's work you're used to. Generous offer. Best you're likely to get."

Boon said nothing. The room was swaying now, reminding him of the waves of heat that came off the ground in the desert.

"Give you time to think it over. Don't try to see her, son."

Bender turned and left him, leaving the door wide-open. Boon swayed, recognizing that stubbornness could only keep him upright for so long, and sank back to the bed.

He wasn't sure how he was going to see Laurie. He only knew he would see her.

Laurie did not recall crawling into the covers or falling asleep. She roused sometime later to find the lamp beside her mattress burning low and the room cast in shadows. Her eyes fixed upon a photograph of her mother in a gilded frame on the side table that held the lamp. Her father still had a photo of his wife beside his pillow, even though she had divorced him.

Voices came from beyond the door, familiar voices. Her parents, she realized. Was that what had roused her? She lifted up on an elbow to hear better. This was not the gentle murmur of conversation, but the escalating pitch of voices raised in anger. She slipped from the sheets and crept across the floor on bare feet, creaking open the door just a crack. Light flooded in and she realized it was morning. Had she slept through the day and night? A glance back confirmed that the heavy velvet curtains were drawn, but light puddled beneath, spilling upon the floor and creeping through the cracks. She turned her attention to her parents.

"You're the one who refused to come to San Antonio. That was your call, not mine." That was her father.

"Because you had turned our daughter into a wild little Indian."

"She could ride and shoot better than most of my men."

"But she was a girl, a young lady, or she should have been."

Something moved beside Laurie and she nearly fainted from fear. She turned to find Paloma, who was likely sent to watch over her while she slept, as she clutched a hand over her mouth at the last moment before screaming.

Paloma pressed a finger to her lips and drew beside her at the door. It was a position they had once often assumed, in the days before her parents split apart.

"I gave her up when you asked me. I let you take her, didn't I?" Her father's voice sounded grieved.

Laurie had never realized her mother had insisted that he relinquish his control over her. She thought back to the hurt and confusion, her body changing, her mind changing and her father's sudden and complete withdrawal. She had thought something was wrong with her.

"But why wouldn't you come when I sent for you? I had a house, like you asked for. What did I do wrong, Valencia?"

"How could we come back?"

"I don't understand."

Her mother heaved a sound of extreme frustration. She then let out a string of Spanish so fast that Laurie caught only the part that compared him in intelligence to a peasant's burro.

"English! Or slow down."

She switched in midsentence. "You! You and your wild Texans. What do you think will happen when you bring them right to your daughter?"

Silence. Paloma now stared at Laurie with the intention of a cat eyeing a tasty little bird.

Her father's voice now held a note of menace. "Spit it out, Val."

"You remember that one, Anton Fischer?"

"Use to ride with me. Quit when he got hitched. Liked to care for the horses. What about him?"

"He liked to care *for your daughter*."

"What!" The sound of her father's boots clomping across the floor caused both Paloma and Laurie to dash toward the far side of the room. But he spun and returned the way he had come.

Laurie stood frozen, clutching the bedrail, her mind whirling like a pinwheel. How had her mother discovered this? Had she known all this time? Was that why they had left Father, because of her, because of what she had done? Her heart beat with a fury that caused a dreadful ache in her chest and she looked to Paloma. Her housekeeper's gaze was steely.

Paloma whispered in Spanish, "You wonder how your mother knows? I told her. Showed her the blood on the underclothes that you tried to hide. I see everything in my house."

Laurie's ears heated. The voices continued and she could not resist. She returned to the door with Paloma, following her like a calf after its mama.

"Did he…" Her father's words fell off.

Silence.

"I'll kill him."

"Yes, I knew you would. And that is why I took our daughter away from you both. That way she is safe and you are not under arrest for murder.

"Anyway, he is gone. I have kept my eye on him. After he left you, he got married but is still a Don Juan. When I heard he was shot in Austin by the father of a Mexican girl, I was not sorry. But I was sorry for the Mexican man, for they hung him."

Laurie staunched most of the gasp that escaped her by clamping a hand over her mouth. She thumped back against the wall beside the door as Paloma's eyes glittered like obsidian as she stared at Laurie.

"Now I fear the same is happening with this one, Boon. Who is he, one of your men?"

"No. Not one of mine." His response was so emphatic that it made Laurie twitch as if her father had slapped her. Boon had been right about this. Her father had used him with no intention of offering Boon a place in his company.

"A private man, then? Someone you hired outside the law, paid for Laurie's safe return?"

This time his no was slower in coming. "Not exactly."

"Then why did that boy ride into an outlaw camp to rescue our daughter?"

Laurie knew why. She had figured out that Boon wanted to be a Texas Ranger. She wondered if her father knew that was why he went. Had her father taken advantage of a man who obviously looked up to him?

Her mother continued her interrogation, proving she might have made a fine peace officer herself. "Had he prior knowledge of her?"

"None."

Valencia's voice held irritation. "Was it, perhaps, because the great and influential Captain John Bender asked him to go? And they were alone, how long? What did he do to her, Johnny?"

"Just what you fear he did, Vallie."

Her mother gave a shriek of aggravation.

"He said she was a virgin and he took her."

Laurie held her breath in the silence. Boon had lied for her. It gave her a moment's hope.

Her mother spoke at last. "He is protecting her then. This is trouble brewing. She needs to be married soon and to a man who will stay put. Not a cowboy or a lawman."

Laurie sagged against the wall. They would not turn her out because of her wicked behavior. Her relief lasted only until she realized they meant to marry her off to the first man they could find. Boon. She had to get to Boon and tell him. Her shoulders sagged. He couldn't save her, not from this. Her condition was her own fault. He had done his job, seen her safe.

Her mother spoke again. "Sooner is better."

"No one knows where she's been."

That growl emerged from her mother again. Only Laurie's father could bring that particular sound from her. "Except the doctor, all of your men, this one, Boon, and anyone who saw her when you brought her in looking as if she'd been dragged behind a wagon for days."

Both Paloma and Laurie craned their necks to hear. Laurie tried to identify the sound, but it was unfamiliar.

Her father's voice was low and gentle now. "Now, Vallie, it will be all right."

Laurie moved to peer out the crack and saw her father holding her mother, his chin tucked over her dark head and her body nearly vanishing in his big, strong arms.

"Vallie, we'll see to her."

"What if there is a child?"

"We'll have to marry her off quick, is all. Then we'll move. I got orders to go to Lubbock."

"Lubbock," moaned Valencia. "It is the Apache Territory."

"It's real nice. You'll like it, Vallie. I swear."

She pulled back. "No. For now we wait and see. If, please God, we come through this, she will marry after an appropriate lapse, so there can be no shadow of doubt."

"And if she don't come through this?"

"Then a quick wedding is the only choice." Valencia turned away, stepping from her father's arms. "What about the outlaw, Boon? You have to send him away, quickly."

"I offered him the reward money to leave town. He wouldn't take it."

"What do you mean, he wouldn't take it?" asked Valencia, incredulity dripping from her words.

"I don't know. He told me to give the reward money to Laurie. Said it was her bullet that killed him."

"Johnny, is that so?"

"Possibly. Coats hit him, too."

Paloma pressed a hand over her heart.

She crossed herself and muttered a prayer against evil.

"You cannot send him off empty-handed," said Valencia. "If you run him off with nothing, he might talk."

"I offered him a job in El Paso with Paul Laskins at the Bar 4, but he turned me down again."

"Well, what *does* he want?"

Laurie knew. She knew and she also knew that she had to help him get it. She couldn't do it, but her father could. Laurie stepped through the door to stand before her parents.

Valencia noticed Laurie first.

"Laura, you are awake." Her voice was gentle but held strain, like the quavering note of a violin string.

Behind her, the captain's expression turned wary and her parents exchanged a look. They were likely wondering how much she had overheard, but neither was willing to ask.

"I thought Paloma would inform me when you woke," said Valencia, looking past Laurie to the darkened chamber beyond, her brows lifted expectantly.

Paloma slunk around the door. Had she had a tail, it would have surely been tucked between her legs.

"Ah, there she is. Will you see about breakfast, please. For three."

Laurie stepped farther into the room that her father used as parlor and office, refusing to ignore the topic that hung about them like oily smoke from a grease fire.

"You want to know what Boon wants?"

She had their attention; both parents stared at her with a mixture of uncertainty and expectation. How she would have loved to tell them that what Boon wanted, what kept him here, was her. But she knew better. He had told her he would leave her upon arrival. And he had told her, indirectly, what his heart desired. Did she have the power to give it to him?

"He wants to become a Texas Ranger," she said.

Her father's answer was instantaneous.

"I'll be damned first."

Laurie held her ground. "He brought me back alive. He did what you asked. He's earned it."

"What he's earned is a short rope and a long drop."

Chapter Eighteen

Laurie's father had treated her like a child, ordering her to her room to dress for breakfast. How had she ever tolerated being ordered about like a servant? She felt as if she were only just arousing from a deep slumber, waking, flexing her muscles and running into the bars of her cage. She had to get out, get away from them both, but how?

Her mother appeared a few minutes later and laid out her second-best dress. The remains of the first had disappeared with Paloma and, she suspected, was now on its way to the ash heap to be burned.

Her mother set the neatly folded pile containing the clean chemise, petticoats and bloomers, the skirt and bodice over the back of one chair.

Laurie stared down at the pink gingham dress with a feeling that it belonged to someone else, some earlier version of Laurie Garcia Bender, who no longer existed. The lace trim and the flounces of fabric that were gathered to cascade down the back of her legs all now seemed impractical, and the color childish.

Paloma returned carrying the crinoline. In her other hand she held a boar's hairbrush and comb.

"The breakfast is here and the captain, he is waiting," said Paloma, thumbing over her shoulder.

Her mother stilled, the brush half the distance between Laurie's crown and shoulders.

"Thank you, Paloma," said her mother. "Do stay and help Laurie with her corset, after which I will not need you until midday."

Laurie watched her mother go, happy for the reprieve. Why was it that she had never found her mother's questions intrusive or her attention cloying until this very minute?

Paloma cinched her up with efficiency that bordered on aggression. Laurie could scarcely draw breath as she stepped into the crinoline and then stood like a diver, hands poised above her head as their housekeeper tossed a series of petticoats over her head and tethered them about her waist. The ordeal was tedious, but soon Laurie looked like a proper young lady once more. She leaned in to study the yellowing bruise on her cheek that Hammer had given her.

Paloma dressed Laurie's hair quickly, creating three braids and then looping and coiling the ropes of hair into a bun at Laurie's nape. By the time Paloma stepped back, Laurie's scalp ached from the tugging.

"Finished," she said in Spanish. Paloma waited for Laurie's approval.

Laurie swept her hand along her head and patted the bun.

"Yes. Thank you."

"Miss Laurie need anything else?"

"Yes. Where did you put the little gun that was in my pocket."

Paloma scowled and held her ground. Laurie arched a brow. The servant spun and rummaged in the bureau, slapping the empty gun on the top. Then she cast one more glare at Laurie before departing, but she did not exit through the door to the adjoining room but directly into the hall. Laurie glanced from one door to the other, alone with her thoughts. It did not take her long to seize the opportunity fate had cast in her path. Her parents may have penned her as neatly as any farm animal but they had also inadvertently left the barn door wide-open.

She rummaged in her trunk and drew out a bonnet, which she hated, for the fabric might be better suited for a baby blanket than a lady's hat, but she took it just the same. She tucked the derringer into a reticule with a lace handkerchief and was out the door without her gloves, tying her bonnet strings as she went.

Laurie searched the hall for Paloma but, seeing no one, she eased into the corridor and gently closed the door. Then she hustled down the hallway as fast as she could manage with each full breath impeded by the restrictive corset. How had she ever managed to wear it before? All the fabrics of her skirts and petticoats rustled in a manner that she now found deeply annoying as she hurried toward the back stairs. The starch in her blouse chafed her skin and the bustle suddenly seemed the most ridiculous invention ever created.

"Laura, where are you going?"

She hunched at her mother's voice and recognized in that instant how Paloma had disappeared so quickly. She'd gone immediately to her mistress.

"Shopping?" Laurie asked.

"I'll just come with you. Wait a moment for me to get my hat."

Boon stood across the street from the Cactus Flower Hotel in San Antonio when he spotted two elegant ladies glide out of the main entrance. Both were stylishly dressed though one held a more sophisticated air in her graceful saunter as she angled her parasol to block the sun. Her companion was slightly taller and dressed in pink, the sort of pink you wrap a baby in. Boon narrowed his eyes as he recognized her face—Laurie. But not Laurie, at least not the Laurie he had known.

She was scrubbed so clean her skin shone and her cheeks glowed a pale pink. Her girlish pink-and-white gingham checked dress made her appear innocent and pure and years younger. Her waist looked impossibly narrow and sculpted. The corset was back, he realized, but where were her gloves?

She was covered from neck to toe, but that dress molded to each curve and hugged her hips like a promise and he wondered how any man could look at her and not want to make her his own.

He stared at the other woman, taking in the similarities and calculating her companion's age. Her mother, he decided.

The two women headed down the boardwalk, step graceful and posture erect. He moved to intercept, crossing their path before they reached the alley beside the hotel. If he were wise he'd light off in the opposite direction. Instead he stepped into the street.

His gaze swept Laurie from head to heel. Her hair was pulled up from her face and her beautiful mane of thick dark hair lay hidden beneath a sunbonnet with a small brim punctuated by a large flower of matching fabric. The bonnet looked as if she might have stolen it from a passing schoolgirl. He grimaced. She already dressed like a preacher's wife.

Neither woman took note of his approach. Why should they? He wasn't anybody worth noticing. Still, he removed his hat.

"Hello, Laurie," he said.

She pulled up short and blinked at him as if he was the very last person she expected to see. He tried a tentative smile but the shock in her eyes killed it. She was like a stranger again.

"Boon! You're out of bed."

He lifted his good arm away from his side. "Appears so."

The other woman stepped between them. "Ah, so this is Mr. Boon. I'm Laura's mother."

Boon detected an accent, a rolling of her words that he recognized as Spanish. He spared her mother a glance and a nod, noting the brittle smile and suspicious eyes. She didn't like this chance meeting, no, not one little bit.

Boon returned his attention to Laurie, who seemed as stiff as the starched lace collar that poked about her throat, and she clutched her reticule in two hands as if afraid he might take it as she cast her gaze at her mother in discomfort.

Who was this woman and where was the Laurie who had ridden like blue blazes in the moonlight? He wanted her back, the woman he loved, the one who rode like a Ranger and defended him from Hammer with all the ferocity of a wildcat. Sadness pierced his heart as he recognized he had lost that woman forever.

He pressed his lips together, determined to try to act like a gentleman, though he knew he'd never be one.

Her smile was gracious. Meanwhile her eyes darted about as if afraid to be seen with him.

"Laura, have you had opportunity to express your thanks to Mr. Boon?" said her mother.

"I will be forever grateful to you," she said, all graciousness and good manners.

He snorted. "You already talk like a Sunday-school teacher."

Laurie's mouth gaped in surprise but her mother never missed a beat.

"And I also thank you," said her mother, "For seeing my daughter home safely."

Boon looked from one to the other feeling sick to his stomach. They'd bound her up again, roped and tied her like a cow for branding. Didn't she see that?

Laurie's brave smile trembled on her lips and then disappeared. He didn't like the new awkwardness between them or the way she shifted from side to side as if in a hurry to be done with him. He hardly blamed her, but it still stung.

Would she miss him at all?

She stared up at him and the zing of attraction fired between them. He couldn't take his eyes off her.

She angled her head to one side as if trying

to find something in his expression. He wished he'd had a chance to shave.

Why did she look at him like that, like some lost puppy? Didn't she know it was all over? Didn't she know where she belonged?

He feared that this might be their last meeting and now he didn't know what to say.

"How are you feeling?" he managed, dancing around the topic of their night together.

She flushed. "Oh. Very well."

"Laura, please. You're delaying this man from his business," said her mother.

"How are *you* feeling?" she echoed, ignoring her mother's admonishment.

"I'm just exactly the same and so are you." He swept a hand before her elaborate getup. Then he leaned out to the side to stare at her posterior. "See you got your bustle back."

Her mother gasped and then snapped her parasol shut. "If you'll excuse us, Mr. Boon," she said, dismissing him. "Come, Laura."

The two stepped past him. He leaned in so they could hear him.

"I still ain't leaving 'til I know," he said.

They both stiffened in unison. Then he watched them walk away, heartsick at the speed Laurie had fallen back into her old life, her old clothes and her old habits. Well, what had he expected, that she'd throw her arms about him and kiss him hello?

Boon pulled his hat low over his eyes and headed in the opposite direction.

Laurie's mother returned them immediately to her husband's hotel room, where Laurie faced her mother's fury. Her mother was certain Laurie had been sneaking out to see Boon. When she finished shrieking at her daughter, Laurie underwent an interrogation that ended when Laurie lost her temper and told her it was none of her business. She was angry and upset but strangely satisfied that she'd stood up to her mother rather than lying to her. She spent the rest of the dreadful day sequestered in her father's chambers until her mother obtained the room across the hall and their belongings were moved. Supper was served in her father's chambers, after which she retired early, just to be alone. It was hard to think, hard to breathe and hard to sit under her parents' constant scrutiny. They watched her as if she might suddenly go mad. They watched her as if they did not know her at all.

Perhaps they didn't. She hardly knew herself. Boon had said she was exactly the same and on the outside, at least, that was true. But inside she was still changing.

Laurie crawled into the unfamiliar bed, her mind restless. She squeezed both hands over her heart and curled into a ball. She must have slept, because she did not hear her mother come into their bed and when Laurie roused, her mother was already up and out. She glanced at the opposite pillow. That was odd. Laurie was nearly always up before her mother. And her mother never made her own bed, but her side of the mattress looked undisturbed. Laurie's eyes narrowed as the suspicion niggled.

She was in no hurry to rise today, so she curled on her side. Her entire body ached. She closed her eyes and lay there with the curtains drawn and the bright fall light stealing across the floor beneath them. She thought of Boon, surprised to see him out of bed. Their meeting had deflated her like a falling cake.

His coldness, his harsh words had cut her like broken glass. Why had he been so dreadful? And why could she not managed to speak to him with her mother standing by watchful as a hawk?

Everything had changed between them, Laurie realized. Boon had become a stranger.

His hard words came back to haunt her, each striking like a blow to her stomach.

You already talk like a Sunday-school teacher.

I see you got your bustle back.

Had he said those things merely to hurt her?

She didn't know. She only knew that they had. The sadness of their last meeting sank deep into her bones.

Her stomach cramped as she accepted that Boon did not want her. All that held him to her was his sense of obligation. If she wasn't with child, he'd leave her. And if she was, he'd stay, but not for any reason of affection. He'd stay because he had vowed not to be like the men who'd used his mother. He would stay out of duty.

Laurie's stomach hurt now. She didn't understand herself. She was safe, she was back with her family and they would take care of her. She didn't need Boon, but somehow, she did.

Laurie rolled to her back on the pillow, her hands fisted in the hair at her temples as she stared up at the headboard with sightless eyes. Understanding dawned, red as any sunrise.

She understood now why her return was joyless and why she could not calm her restless mind. It was not the ordeal she had endured, not the hard treatment or the rough riding or even the magical night she had shared with Boon. No, it was much more than that. Her parents were right to watch her. Right to keep her close. Had they guessed already at what she had only just recognized?

Laurie rolled, the realization bringing her upright on the bed. She stared at her reflection in the mirror, seeing her mouth open in surprise, the pallor of her face and the worry in her eyes.

She knew now why she could not keep herself from touching him on the trail or why she'd yearned to touch him again on the street yesterday.

She loved him.

Laurie groaned. Oh, no. What had she done?

Was she really fool enough to take up with a man who was wild as the west wind, who had no desire to stay with her? Just look what had happened to her mother, abandoned by the one she loved. Laurie needed to find a stable man, someone who would not leave her to go chase Apache or to track rustlers into Mexico. Someone with roots and a business and a home and…

Laurie pressed both hands to her face. Sweet mercy, she'd fallen in love with Boon.

Laurie hugged her knees and rocked. Both her lower back and her stomach ached. She stilled as the clues from her body reached her conscious mind.

"No," she whispered.

Laurie threw back the covers, twisting to look at the bedding and the back of her nightdress. Both were stained with her blood.

Chapter Nineteen

If you get your monthly you're clear. If not, well, we got business. Boon's words echoed in Laurie's mind. So they no longer had business. Laurie pressed a hand to her mouth, realizing that the last thread connecting them had broken. He was now free. She was free. Free to face the rest of her life without him.

"No, no, no!" The words were a chant, a prayer, a cry of mourning.

She pressed the heels of her hands into her eye sockets to keep from weeping.

She knew she had again escaped the consequences of her folly. But this time hadn't been folly. Her lovemaking with Boon had felt right, natural, wonderful. And her bleeding served only to add to her misery.

Laurie rose to wash herself, when Paloma appeared with a breakfast tray.

She took one look at Laurie and the bloodstained bedding and laid the tray aside, retreating without a word.

Laurie's mother arrived shortly afterward with the folded linen pads, still wearing the dress Laurie had seen her wearing last night.

"So, you are not with child," said Valencia Sanchez Garcia with a pretty smile upon her face as if the news was wonderful instead of tragic.

Laurie shook her head.

Her mother took her in her arms. "Now you can forget him and he may be on his way. And in any case, this means there is no urgency for you to marry. It would be wise to wait at least six months so there will be no speculation."

"I do not even have a suitor," Laurie protested, feeling suddenly as if she were on a runaway horse, careening down a steep incline.

Her mother continued as if Laurie had not spoken. "We will be moving to Lubbock, to your father's new assignment."

"But what about Calvin?" The reason Laurie had gone to San Antonio in the first place was because her mother had announced her intention to marry Calvin.

"He has his business in Austin and I have business here with you and your father. It seems fairly obvious that you need my full attention. And in Lubbock, you can have a fresh start. Your father has agreed to help find a suitable match."

"But I don't want a suitable match." She wanted Boon.

Her mother drew back and narrowed her eyes upon her daughter. "Laura Garcia Bender, do not tell me that you believe yourself in love with this man. He is a drifter and a criminal. You'll not be seeing him again."

Laurie locked her jaw. She might not be able to hold Boon here, but she would at least say goodbye.

"Now you rest a bit. I'll have Paloma bring you some chamomile tea."

Her mother moved toward the door.

"Are you going to see father?" asked Laurie.

Valencia paused at the door. "Yes, but I will return shortly."

Her mother walked across the hallway to find her husband in a discussion with Sam Coats. Both men stood at her appearance and then Coats excused himself, leaving the room.

As soon as they were alone she reported Laurie's condition to him.

"Now you need to send him away," she said. "Far away, for Laurie has crazy ideas about that one. I know my daughter and she can be as stubborn as you sometimes."

Captain Bender rose and reached for his hat. "I'll see to it."

Shortly after leaving Valencia, Captain Bender reached Dr. Langor's office to discover that Boon had moved to a boardinghouse over on the other side of the tracks.

Boon sensed someone watching him as he was finishing his breakfast in the common dining area. He glanced about and met Captain John Bender's steady blue eyes. Boon wiped his mouth and followed him out onto the porch of Mrs. Sheffield's rooming house.

"Been thinking on you, son."

Boon could only imagine that Bender's thoughts had leaned toward murder.

Bender did not mince words. "Laurie is bleeding, so she's not with child, lucky for you."

Boon stared in silence, absorbing the news. To his credit, the captain did not look smug. Captain Bender was many things: fierce, protective, smart and a fearless fighter. What he was not was a liar. If he said Laurie was not with child, Boon believed him.

"You satisfied?" asked the captain.

Boon drew a heavy breath and then gave a single nod of his head.

"Then you're free to go, unless you changed your mind about that reward money."

"Nope."

Bender cast him a long speculative look. Boon wondered what he was thinking.

"Too bad I didn't get to hang Hammer. That's what all outlaws deserve." Bender's voice was congenial, as if they were now old friends. It put Boon further on edge.

"Outlaws like me?" asked Boon.

"Son, when we took you, you didn't even have a gun. You were their prisoner, same as Laurie. That's why I didn't hang you. You were an innocent man."

"I'm a killer."

Bender held his gaze. "We're all killers, son. Me, Coats, the rest of my Rangers. Some men just need killing. You were fighting for your life and for Laurie's. I can square with that. You done real good, son." Bender squeezed his uninjured shoulder. Boon had once lived for such a show of affection and approval. Now it felt hollow and not nearly as important. Laurie had changed him right down to the core and he feared he'd never be able to be that man he'd once longed to become. Was there any way to have them both, the respect of this man and the love of his daughter? No, he decided. He'd burned that bridge good and proper.

"So all that's left is for us to settle up," said Bender.

Boon braced for another blow but Bender only reached in his pocket, drawing something out which he held in his fist. He extended his hand, uncoiling his fingers. There in his palm lay the only thing Boon had ever really coveted—a shiny Mexican peso cut into a Ranger's badge. Across the middle the letters had been stamped and then blackened so they could be easily read: Texas Ranger.

Boon's heart started pumping like a piston as he looked to the captain for confirmation.

"It's yours, son. You earned it."

Boon reached. The captain closed his fist, removing the prize. Boon's arm dropped back to his side as elation ebbed against the incoming wave of suspicion. No one had ever given him something for nothing, so what was the catch?

"But just one thing," said the captain. "I

won't be your commander. You'll be working under Robert Hart down in McAllen. Mostly trouble with bandits and rustlers."

McAllen. If it were any farther south he'd be in Mexico. In fact, you could see Mexico from the banks of the Rio Grande.

"I think you'll understand when I tell you that you are exactly the sort of man I'd like as one of my men. But not the kind I'd choose for my Laurie. She needs someone steady, someone who's gonna stay put and not get himself shot chasing rustlers. You're too damned much like me."

Boon agreed with him there. But if the captain was forcing a choice, Boon was sure he wouldn't like the outcome. He wasn't keen on being offered the badge as a bribe to keep clear of his daughter. Still he didn't see that he had any choice in the matter.

"I understand, sir."

Bender's mustache twitched in what might have passed for a smile and then he slapped the badge down into Boon's palm, following the exchange with a handshake that kept the warm metal star suspended between them.

Boon slowly shook his head. He met the captain's puzzled expression and held his gaze.

"Coats was right. I ain't Ranger material."

Boon set the badge on the top of the porch rail, tapping it once in farewell. "And as for Laurie…"

Bender's expression turned from cordial to deadly but Boon forged on.

"As for Laurie, she's too much of a lady to fall for the likes of me. So I'll be heading out."

The captain's exhalation seemed to hold a good deal of relief. That surprised Boon. Did her father really think his daughter was a fool? Laurie might have had a fancy for him, but she'd come to her senses with time.

"Where you headed, son?"

"Don't know, exactly. I'm free as the summer wind. Might see which way it blows me. I hear there's gold in the Black Hills."

"Raiding Sioux up there, too."

"No one lives forever."

Bender's mustache twitched in what might have been a smile.

Boon headed for the livery where he'd boarded the ponies he'd stolen from Hammer for the cost of one of their saddles.

He needed to get clear of San Antonio, this man, this whole damn city. He wondered how far would be far enough to put Laurie behind him.

Chapter Twenty

Laurie dressed and then announced that she would see Boon. Her mother ordered her to stay in the hotel, but not even her mother's ire would sway her. She wanted to see him and this time she would tell him that she loved him. She pushed past her mother and left the hotel.

Since she did not know where to find Boon, she retraced their steps, deciding that Dr. Langor would likely know where Boon could be found. She had reached the doctor's office and was just lifting her hand to knock when her father caught up with her.

"Laurie!"

She turned and saw the captain, approaching at a fast walk.

"Laurie, why you out here alone?" Her father glanced at her raised hand, poised to knock on the doctor's door. Then he stared at her midsection. "Something wrong with you?"

She blinked, unsure how to answer. There was so very much wrong with her at the moment.

"Did you see Boon?" she asked.

"Yes."

Her father reached for her now, taking firm hold of her elbow and turning them about.

"Come on," he ordered.

If he wanted a fight, she would give it to him. Laurie lifted her chin in defiance. "I am not your hound."

"You're my girl."

He hadn't called her that in years.

"I used to be. But I am not yours any more than I am a girl."

"I don't know why you had to go and grow up anyways," he grumbled, rubbing the back of his neck with his opposite hand, which sent his hat tipping forward.

She almost felt sorry for him. John Bender was competent in many areas, but raising a daughter was clearly not one of them. Did he feel uncertain as to his decisions regarding her?

"Well, I have grown up, very recently in

fact. Father, do you know why I came to be on that train?"

His eyes grew cautious, but he did not answer.

"I was trying to find you. I hoped that telling you about mother would bring you home. I truly believed that if I went to you and explained what was happening that you would swoop in, like you used to, and make everything all right."

Bender released Laurie and his mustache drooped with his mouth.

"A week ago, I believed that your divorce had ruined my life. That I couldn't find a suitor because of it. But the truth is that I cast off every man that got near me. I'd think of Anton Fischer and freeze up inside like the Great Plains in February."

Her father's eyes narrowed and he cast a glance about. For a moment he looked as if he needed rescuing.

"I've been afraid of every single man that's come near me, except Boon, but he won't have me without your approval because he thinks I'm too much of a lady. Well, we both know that's not so."

Her father tried unsuccessfully to set them in motion. Laurie dug in her heels.

"Do you recall the day you told me that it was unladylike to ride a horse?"

He stopped at her side, glaring fiercely.

Laurie continued. "When you said a lady might carry a derringer in her bag, but not a holster strapped to her hip? We stopped riding together that day."

He lowered his head as if ashamed, but that was wrong. Her father had never felt shame, never apologized for anything. And up until today, she had never suspected that he was uncertain about his decision to leave them.

Her father's voice held a note of strain when he spoke. "Your mother said that you were a distraction to my men, flying across the territory with your skirts up and your hair trailing behind you. You needed some education."

"You taught me."

"That was when you were a girl. When you grew up, it was no longer proper."

"So you sent us away."

"Your mother thought it best. She said she needed to get hold of you before you turned out just like Calamity Jane. That woman could drive an eight-mule team even after she drank a full bottle of grain alcohol. But I can see your mother's point."

Laurie had never known that, but she knew they argued over her upbringing.

"Hell, I don't know what's best for a young lady. That is your mother's area of expertise. So I gave you up."

"So I could put on corsets, put up my hair, start wearing gloves and bonnets? Lavender powder, satin ribbons? Do you know why I did all that?"

"Because it is the proper thing."

Laurie shook her head. "Because you told me that you wanted me to grow into a proper lady. That you expected me to do just as Mother said and put away my rifle and the rubber waders I used for fishing and so I did. Just like that, because you asked it. I did everything you wanted and all to please you. But you never came back. I believed you were checking on me. Wondered who among the town folks was your agent. It took me a long time to realize that no one was."

"I was working to provide for you and your mother."

"I gave up everything I loved for you." She tore off her bonnet with such force it toppled her carefully styled hair. A shower of hairpins bounced off the planking like hail. "And I won't do it again." She pulled off her gloves and threw them down to the porch boards between them.

"Laurie! What the Sam Hill are you doing?"

She'd never seen her father look uncertain before, but she saw it now, that shifting of his eyes, the search for rescue and then the bewilderment when he realized that he'd have to face her alone.

"I won't be a proper lady any longer." She reached back and removed the combs, untying the ribbons, letting her dark hair fall down her back. "I am more like you than I am like Mother. I do not want to sit with embroidery. I want to ride and shoot and live. Why do the men get to have all the adventures while the women have to perch, like birds, in stifling hot parlors in corsets that hold us so tight we cannot draw a full breath?"

Her father released her and backed away. Laurie advanced.

"Do you remember the snake skin we found? I kept it. It's tucked away in a cigar box at home with all the other improper things I've hidden." Laurie lifted her hand and ticked off the list. "My throwing knife, the deck of cards you used to teach me poker, the horse pick, jaw harp and the last pack of Black Jack chewing gum you bought me because ladies must not chew gum."

"Laurie, you stop it now. You hear?" Her father's voice did not hold its usual authority. Instead it held a certain note of panic.

"No." She stepped forward. "No more. I have had my fill of bustles and corsets and ridiculous hats that do not even keep the sun from my face. I have had enough of tiny uncomfortable shoes and reading poetry. I am my father's daughter and I will not allow you or anyone else to dictate to me."

His face turned red as he aimed a finger at her. "You'll do as we say."

Laurie pulled back. "No, sir. You lost that right when you sent me away and made me ashamed of what I was. From now on, I make my own decisions and I will ride astride and shoot and I'll drink whiskey if I like. I will be a proper lady no more!"

Her father's eyes narrowed.

"Now tell me where he is," she ordered.

"He's leaving. Might be gone already."

The fight left Laurie so fast it turned her knees to jelly. Laurie swayed, her mission suddenly becoming imperative. If she didn't find him, didn't catch him, she might never see him again.

Her father grasped her wrist but she wrenched away.

"Laurie?" Her father's eyes were wide with concern.

"Where?" she whispered.

He didn't answer.

"Where!" This time her words were a shout.

"Sheffield's boardinghouse. Happy? Now let's go."

Her father made a grab for her but she upended a chair on Dr. Langor's porch and then threw herself over the railing while he tangled on it, giving her time to run. She lifted her skirts and bolted down the street as fast as her legs would carry her.

Laurie stopped only for directions to Sheffield's but upon reaching the house she discovered that Boon had departed after speaking with her father.

Desperate, she hurried to the livery as directed by Mrs. Sheffield and found Boon headed for the office with one of the three saddles they used slung over his shoulder.

He spotted her a moment later and paused. He dropped the saddle, raising a cloud of dust.

"Come to shout good riddance?" He tried to joke but his heart hurt and his throat felt tight.

He took a good look at her, seeing she was

panting, pale, with perspiration beading on her brow. Her hair was flying about her face and she had no gloves. Where was her bonnet?

"Laurie, what in tarnation?"

He untied his neckerchief and used it to wipe her brow. He couldn't resist letting his index finger stroke her soft cheek in the process. Laurie gasped and sputtered a moment and he drew her to the shade of the eaves.

She leaned in and lifted both hands, reaching for his face, but he stepped back. Was she crazy, trying to caress him right out here on the street? If Laurie wouldn't see to her reputation, he'd have to.

"Your folks know you're out here alone?"

She didn't answer.

"Go on back to them, Laurie-gal."

"I had to see you."

So she had been on her way to find him, seeking him out. Lord Almighty, the woman lacked all sense.

"Well, you seen me. I'm right as rain." Except he was still seeing double and he couldn't lift one arm.

She glanced about again as if expecting pursuit, then met his gaze with those big dark eyes that caused him to melt inside.

"I am sorry about before, with my mother.

I didn't know what to say or do." She peeked up at him from beneath dark, thick lashes and he knew for certain his heart was gone. Lord, he'd never get over her.

He checked himself. This gal stirred him up like dust before a thunderstorm, his rainmaker, but he'd already caused her enough anguish. He'd not make it worse. Her parents were right to tuck her away like the prize that she was and keep her safe until they could find someone who deserved her. If not for that one night together, he'd already be gone.

Lord, what was she doing talking to the likes of him?

"I was so worried when you had that fever. I feared losing you."

"Well, I thought that was the idea. You never planned on keeping me, Laurie. I ain't the keeping kind."

"You could be."

She looked up at him with wide expectant eyes. He needed to put an end to this, for his good as well as hers.

His heart squeezed with a pain that took him totally unawares. He ached to have her and to have a child by her.

"Hell."

Laurie blinked in surprise and he recalled

belatedly that men didn't say damn or hell to ladies.

"Do you remember what you told me? Do I look like a banker or a preacher to you?"

"If you were, I'd be dead right now," she said. "You saved me."

He threaded his hands through the hair at his temples, trying again to do what was right.

"Your pa told me," he said. "You come through all right?"

She flushed and nodded her head. "This morning," she confirmed. Her eyes welled with tears. "Don't leave me."

"Laurie," he said, his voice chiding. "How did you think this would end? Did you think your ma and pa would be happy to have their daughter fall for a no-account drifter who's ridden with the worst outlaw in the entire state of Texas?"

"They don't know you."

He locked his jaw, not wanting to do what he must. Wishing to savor the moment when Laurie Bender wanted him as much as he yearned for her.

"Oh, Laurie," he choked, longing to give in to the fantasy.

"Stay with me, Boon."

He almost said yes. But he loved her too

much to stay. Too much to watch her lose everything. Too much to saddle her with the likes of him.

"You're not hitching your wagon to mine. I've got no land, no livelihood. Hell, I don't even have a last name to give you. So here's how it is—I'm going. You're staying."

"But I love you," she whispered.

He closed his eyes against the joy and agony. How could he ever have hoped to win the love of such a woman?

She tried to kiss him but he held her off with one hand.

"No, you don't. You can't. I won't let you. Your ma and pa are right. You listen to them and marry a man who can give you all the things you deserve."

"But I want you."

"No."

She looped her arms about his neck, looking at him with welling eyes, and he felt his heart turn to dust. She'd never forgive him for what he was about to do and that was best for all concerned.

He dragged her arms from his neck and pushed her roughly aside. "Laurie, you aren't my type. I'm used to good-time girls, not some prim, priggish woman who's as starched as her corset stays."

Laurie staggered as if he had punched her. But still she didn't go. He reached down deep, lifting one last stone, the one he knew would drive her off and still he hesitated, hating to throw it.

"Boon," she whispered. "Stay."

He shook his head and threw the rock. "I never stay anywhere. You come with me and I'll leave you upstairs in some saloon, which is probably where you belong."

She stared in horror. "But you said…you said it didn't matter. That any man worth his salt would choose a woman for what is on the inside."

He scooped up the saddle. "Oh, hell, Laurie. I'd have said anything to get you on that horse and moving."

It took another moment for Laurie to whirl and run back the way she had come, her skirts flying out behind her, leaving him time to contemplate a life without her.

Laurie was too good for him. Always was, always would be.

Chapter Twenty-One

Laurie pressed a hand over her aching heart as she staggered back toward the hotel. How was it still beating? she wondered.

Paloma found her first, just after she reached the porch of the hotel.

"Your parents are out searching for you. They left me in case you came home."

Laurie's vision blurred. Her head pounded. She allowed Paloma to steer her through the lobby and up the stairs; all the while the sound of a locomotive roared in her head.

"Do you hear that?" she shouted, holding her hands to her ears, but the sound just got louder. Laurie looked at Paloma's troubled expression and the edges of her vision darkened until she could see only a small circle of twinkling light. Her stomach pitched and she felt herself falling. She could do nothing but surrender to the darkness.

She woke in her mother's room, the quilt tucked under her chin and her mother sitting guard beside her bed. Laurie blinked.

"He's gone," she whispered. "He left me. He's gone."

Her mother nodded and Laurie closed her eyes again, unwilling to face the ripping heartache that tore her insides out.

"I thought if I told him. I thought..." What? That if she was in love with him that he would magically want to stay? Laurie squeezed her eyes shut at the understanding that he had done exactly what he had told her he would do from the start, that he had no intention of settling down.

"Laurie, *mi hija?*" Her mother sounded far away.

The smelling salts brought her back around. She lay in the same bed, but the doctor was there.

"Here she is, back again. You're giving your parents quite a scare."

Laurie did not speak, but just looked out the window, wishing she could fly after Boon like a sparrow.

At the other side of the room, the three conversed in low tones. *Is it normal? Great shock. A result of recent happenings. Time and rest, quiet.* Their words melted together and she closed her eyes to sleep. Anything to escape the hollowness that yawned inside her.

Over the next few weeks Laurie slept much, ate little and worried her parents greatly. She had no energy, she had no appetite and she could not seem to do more than sit and stare.

Her mother tried to coax her with her favorite foods, visitors, consultations with the doctor. Walks were suggested, so every day Laurie was walked up the street and down. While she moved, her body felt as if it were packed in cotton, insulated and apart from everything around her.

In the second month since her return, her parents announced that they planned to remarry.

Laurie smiled at the irony. At one time, their reunion was all she ever wanted. Her certainty that their separation had been the only obstacle between her and happiness had been absolute. How naive she had been. She was unwed because she could not see herself as a worthy wife. Now she just felt sad.

Laurie's mother filled her daughter's day

with endless projects, certain that routine would restore her to her former self. But she was wrong. Her former self was gone forever, dead and buried. But still, here she sat flipping through a copy of *Peterson's Ladies National Magazine* for an idea for a suitable dress to wear to her parents' second wedding when she stumbled upon a riding outfit that included a pair of voluminous pantaloons designed to cover a woman's legs when she rode astride. It was the newest fashion, popular among lady equestrians and women of the West, said one of the fashion articles. The garment was actually a skirt, sewn with a split up the middle. When standing or walking, a woman appeared to be wearing a proper skirt and it was only when she mounted a horse that one could see the nonconformity.

Laurie's mother noticed her interest and peered at the page.

"They're fairly scandalous," she said.

"I'm going to make them," said Laurie.

Her mother indulged her, possibly because it had been a long time since Laurie had showed an interest in anything.

Laurie had a pair fashioned out of sturdy denim by the next evening and tried them on the following day. Riding out and away from town gave her the first pleasure she'd experienced since Boon's departure. Her father accompanied her, making her nostalgic.

When Arlene Juliet approached her later that same week, Laurie expected it was to give her a good talking-to, but instead, the wife of the general store owner wanted to see about purchasing the garment for herself and also commission several pairs for the store.

Her mother disapproved of her daughter working like a servant, but Captain Bender overruled her. Had he listened when she said she would be a proper lady no more? Was he actually helping her?

Over the next month Laurie discarded her corset and bustle. She went riding with her father, taking a rifle along and proving to still be a very good shot. She sewed in the evening, creating the pantaloons and later a split-back canvas duster, similar to the ones the men wore when riding, but fitted to a woman's form and including a hood that could be tied beneath the chin like a bonnet. These, too, proved popular and Laurie had to hire help to keep up with demand.

In the third month, suitors began to arrive. It was as if she had turned on a tap, and suddenly a flood of men descended on her, all eager to convince her to be their wife. She suspected her head for business had much to do with it.

Her mother said it came from her new confidence that somehow showed past her rather unladylike behavior. Men seemed to be drawn to her newfound self-assurance.

Laurie recognized that she now had everything she had once thought she ever wanted, and knowing that made her miserable.

Laurie turned the men away one by one, adding to her mother and father's dismay.

Her parents' wedding was small but lovely. Laurie wore her pink gingham dress, having been too busy with work to make anything else. It was the first time she had worn a corset since her nervous collapse. At the reception, Laurie tried to pretend she was happy, but she feared she did not fool them.

After the wedding supper and before the newly reunited couple departed on their honeymoon to Galveston, her parents drew her aside.

At first, she feared they would not leave, as both were concerned by the changes in her. But she was fine—healthy and, if she was not happy, she was at least content.

Her mother had tried and failed to encourage her to accept any of the suitors who had taken a fancy to her. Her father had also tried to talk some sense into her. Neither could accept that she did not wish to marry. Not any longer, not when she knew what it was to feel passion. Boon's leaving had cut her deep. Her parents thought she just needed time. Laurie knew otherwise. There wasn't another man in the world who could take Boon's place in her heart.

"Laurie, *mi hija,*" began her mother. "We have some news."

The worry in her mother's eyes brought her to alertness. Her father's grim expression heightened her worry.

"We mentioned that we will be moving to Lubbock, to be closer to your father's latest assignment."

Laurie nodded.

"We will be going upon our return from Galveston."

"I'll be staying here," said Laurie.

Her mother gasped. "But, Laurie, you're still welcome in our home. You know that."

"I do. But I want my own home."

Her father shook his head. "A woman shouldn't live alone."

"But I will, just the same."

The two of them exchanged a look. Since

their reunion, they were very good at this silent exchange.

She saw her parents to their train and waved them goodbye. Afterward she returned to the hotel and packed her belongings, moving into the room Boon had vacated at Mrs. Sheffield's boardinghouse. Before her parents returned from their second honeymoon she had made enough money to buy her own sewing machine.

They tried and failed to convince, cajole or browbeat her into accompanying them to Lubbock. She liked her independence too much to ever give it up to live under her parents' roof again.

She wrote them and she worked. On Saturdays she rented a horse, went riding and practiced her shooting. Gene Freeman from the mercantile tried to accompany her but she sent him off. She turned down invitations from several other men and also the invitations from women to have tea or join various ladies' organizations.

Her parents invited her for Christmas. She declined, and so they came to her. She joined them for dinner at the Cactus Flower Hotel, but resisted yet another attempt to have her return with them. She asked after Paloma and was told she was still in Lubbock.

Her mother's efforts to engage Laurie in conversation were painful, but Laurie answered their questions honestly.

"Is there someone here?" asked her mother. "Someone special?"

Laurie almost laughed. There was only one someone special and they had chased him off. No, that wasn't true. She had told Boon how she felt and he had still left her, just as he had foretold. Why was it, after all this time, that just the thought of him made her heart ache as if pressed through a wringer? She hadn't forgotten him, couldn't forget. The anger at his leaving her had gone, but the sadness clung like tar. If she knew where he was, she'd go after him in a minute.

"Are you still pining for that boy?" asked her mother.

Laurie's heart quickened and she glanced away.

"Have you heard from him?" her mother asked.

Laurie fixed her attention on her mother. "No. Have you?"

"Laurie, dear, well, we'd thought that after some time had passed you'd come to your senses and that your feelings for him would diminished somewhat. Have they?" Her mother held her brows raised in a hopeful expression.

This time she did not avoid her mother's gaze, but stared directly. "I love him."

Her mother sighed and then turned to her husband. "Tell her."

Her father's mouth turned grim. "Give her time."

"No. Enough. She's sad. She's thin. So tell her, please."

They knew. Somehow they knew where to find him. Laurie clutched the lapel of her father's new coat.

"Is he all right?"

Her mother nodded and Laurie felt the sweet rush of air into her lungs, sweeping in with the relief. Laurie released her father and closed her eyes, offering up a prayer of thanks. He was alive.

"What happened to him?" she asked, feeling the first true welling of emotion since she fell into a faint after Boon's departure.

"I offered him a Ranger's badge, but he turned me down."

"Turned you down? I don't understand. Boon wanted desperately to be a Ranger."

"He said he didn't take orders well and he was heading to the Dakotas."

Laurie's eyes widened. The Black Hills were notorious for hostile Indians and boomtowns. The lawlessness of that territory was common knowledge. Could she find him there?

"Where in the Dakotas?"

Her mother and father flashed another meaningful look between them. Her mother nodded and her father spoke.

"He's in Colorado."

"But you said..."

"He lied to me or he changed his mind. Might be he didn't want you tracking him. In any case, I ran him down. He is the new sheriff of a mining town in the Rockies."

Laurie's eyes brightened.

"Where?" she whispered half-afraid to hear, fearful of the hope that welled inside her.

"Now, Laurie, I don't know much else. He might be..." Her father didn't finish because she repeated her question. "Town's called Silver Cliff and it's wild as Northwest Texas."

"I'm going." She turned but her mother stepped before her.

"Why don't we just wire him and let him know you're still available?"

Laurie shook her head. "I'm going, just as soon as I can pack."

Her mother gave her husband a beseeching look.

"I'll bring you myself," said the captain. "I just need to wire Coats."

Laurie would have none of it. The following day she was on a train heading west.

Chapter Twenty-Two

Boon walked along the main street of Silver Cliff, past the sea of unfamiliar faces. More arrived each day from the railhead and by mule team, drawn to the grayish mud that turned out to be 75 percent silver ore.

Six thousand by last count and he'd already had to hire five deputies. He passed a lady with dark hair and smiled, tipping his hat.

"Morning, Sheriff," she said.

He liked to be called sheriff. He found deep satisfaction in protecting these people, in providing the kind of order absent from the early part of his life.

But there was a hole in his heart. He'd gotten himself a reputation for avoiding the women in the red-light district and giving more than one of them train fare home. When he began avoiding the respectable women's tentative approach, he became a puzzle. Rumors included that he was married already and that a bullet wound had rendered him incapable. That last one made him laugh. He was physically capable, but he just couldn't get past the dark-haired gal who hailed from Texas. Had she moved on without him? Did she have a banker for a husband? It hurt him to think on her, but his mind just kept running along the same old track.

He wanted her happy, didn't he? Wasn't that why he left? Still, he was one step closer to respectability. He'd never be her match, never be a banker or a preacher. But he was learning his letters, thanks to the help of Mr. Eli Evans, the headmaster of the school. Boon imagined being able to write well enough to send Laurie a letter, ask her how she was faring and if she now had everything she wanted. But the daydream always ended with her not writing back or telling him she was married and expecting a child. It kept him from writing, that and the fact that his lettering still looked as wobbly as a sick chicken.

But he'd found a job as a lawman on his own. He'd not used the reference that Bender had offered him. It wasn't a Ranger, but he had camaraderie with his deputies and it looked like he might even get reelected.

"Justice?"

Boon turned to find Sam Gardner, one of the town council, heading toward him. When he'd arrived and applied for the position as deputy they'd asked his name and then his Christian name and he'd said, "Just is Boon," and somehow that had become Justice Boon. The name stuck and he'd come to accept it.

He even got used to attending church on Sundays. The singing was nice, though he could do without the lecture.

Gardner was telling him that council had approved the cost of patrols to accompany the ore from the mine to the railhead, when Boon noticed a dark-headed woman and turned to stare. He always noticed the ones with black hair, couldn't help himself. He kept looking for Laurie in every face, even when he knew he was a fool for doing so.

This woman was medium height like Laurie and her hair color was right, though her hair was done up in a bun at her nape, instead of flying about her shoulders as he recalled her. She wore a wide hat, but not the fancy ladies' sort. This was more sombrero than bonnet, practical, and reminded him of the hats the cowpunchers wore in Texas. He'd never seen a woman wear such a covering. His brow quirked as he noted the canvas duster she wore over her dress. It was fitted in the bodice and trimmed with black ribbon so it almost looked like a military jacket.

He'd seen similar ones worn by ladies traveling on the Wells Fargo to keep the dust from ruining their clothing. Her hat kept him from seeing her face, but his heart gave a jump and would not listen to the reason of his mind. What would she be doing here in Colorado? Garner noticed his inattention and turned to stare.

"You know her?" asked the councilman.

Boon was about to shake his head no because he did not recognize the confident stride of this woman or the straight, upright posture of a female at ease with her surroundings. This was unusual by any standards. He was intrigued. Who was she?

She was heading right for them.

"Fine-looking woman," said Gardner.

Boon felt the jolt of recognition and his heart set off like a bird released from its cage a moment before remembering that it couldn't be Laurie. Not here.

Likely the woman had spotted his badge, displayed upon his vest, because she needed the sheriff.

Still his feet were in motion. He could see her smile now, but not her eyes. He jogged the final twenty feet and found himself standing in the road before a covered walkway. She lifted her chin and revealed her dark flashing eyes.

"Laurie?" he whispered, not believing what he saw, not willing to hope that she was really here.

Her eyes glittered and her smile was bright, but her chin trembled.

"What are you doing here?" He reached, but remembered that she was not his and let his hands drop to his sides.

Her voice was sweet and familiar. "I came to see you."

He stared in bewilderment.

"Me?" he asked.

The first flicker of unease showed on her face. "I've missed you, Boon."

He glanced about. "Where is your family?" Surely she hadn't come all this way alone.

"I left them back in Texas. I've been living on my own for several months now."

He stepped up beside her and offered her his elbow. She took it, looping her arm in his, and he led her…where, he'd didn't know, but he'd be damned if he'd let the gawkers listen to this conversation. They strolled along as if old friends, when in fact he felt nervous and hopeful all at once. He actually felt sick to his stomach with the hope and worry spilling about inside him.

"I see you're sheriff." She paused and turned before him.

They'd reached the end of the walkway and would have to descend to the street, which was dusty and sprinkled with manure.

"Yup, been so for several months." Was she married? Engaged? He wanted to ask, but instead he just stood there staring, wishing, dying.

"Boon, I have a confession to make."

Here it comes, he thought, his whole body tense with dread.

She rested a bare hand upon his chest. Where were her fancy white gloves?

"I've missed you," she said. "When you left, it nearly killed me. You shouldn't have gone."

"I did it for you."

"No, you did it because you couldn't believe that I loved you, even though I told you so. Instead, you decided it was better to be noble and break your heart and mine."

Boon had pictured seeing Laurie again, but in none of his imaginings did she tear into him like this.

"You wanted to be a lawman and so you have become one, with no help from anyone. I've already heard that you are performing your responsibilities with fairness and competence, Justice." She smiled.

"Oh, Laurie, that just sort of happened."

"I like it," she said. "It suits you."

He mustered his courage. "So you aren't married?"

She snorted. "You are such an aggravating man! No, I'm not married. I told you I loved you. Did you think leaving me would change that? Did you think that I'd just forget and take up with some, some…"

"Banker?" he supplied.

She threw up her hands. "Boon, when I said that I was still a child. But I've grown up."

"Only a few months ago," he said.

"A lifetime," she countered. "I am no longer interested in marrying a man for his profession or the color of his eyes or because I hope to earn respect through him. A woman would be as big a fool to marry for respect as a man would be to choose a bride for her innocence."

She'd taken the words he'd said before leaving and twisted them somehow. He stared, taking in the differences along with what remained familiar. Laurie's new confidence shone like polished silver.

"You are the first person who has ever understood me and the only one who allows me to be myself," she said. "I am done with pretending to be something I am not. And I miss you. So I've come to ask…" Her voice trailed off and she swallowed hard, squaring her shoulders as if readying herself for a blow. "I am here to ask if you have any feelings for me?"

Could it be true? Could she really be here for him?

She lifted a bare hand and stroked his cheek. He closed his eyes at the sweetness of her touch and clenched his jaw against the sweeping arousal that jolted him like lit gunpowder. He couldn't stop himself from capturing her hand and holding it as he opened his eyes to see that she was really still there.

"I was wrong about everything," she whispered. "You are the best man I ever met and I'm not letting you go without a fight."

She moved closer, fingers stroking his face, her thumb brushing his lower lip. She moved to stand before him, her hands gliding down his neck and then his shirt until her right hand covered the silver star pinned on his vest. Then she rested her head against him. But when she spoke, it was not in a whisper. It was with words loud enough for every passerby to hear. She did not hesitate or falter, just spoke from her heart.

"I love you, Justice Boon, and I can't live without you."

Boon almost took her up in his arms. He believed her, saw the changes she spoke of, but still there was one hurdle.

"Your father?" asked Boon.

"Is shocked and I do not care what he thinks. He's getting used to the idea that I have my own mind and do not take orders like one of his men." Laurie lifted her head and gazed up at him as her fingers curled about the lapels of his vest to give him a little shake. "I choose you. And I'd fight them all to have you."

His eyes closed and he gathered Laurie up against him. He could care for her now. He had a job, a home and the respect of this community.

She had given herself to him. The sweet relief poured down on him like spring rain, followed by the raw need for possession. She was his at last.

She clung to him as he cradled her in the safety of his arms.

"Is it true?" he whispered.

She nodded, her eyes welling with tears. He let her draw back to arm's length.

No one had ever been willing to fight for him. No one had ever really loved him before. He knew he did not deserve her, even now. But he loved her. That was the only explanation for leaving her behind.

"You sure about this?"

She was and did not hesitate. "Completely."

"Laurie, I don't know what I ever did to deserve you, but I know I'm not strong enough to let you go twice."

"That will save me the trouble of coming to fetch you again."

"I'd like to stay here if you're willing."

She glanced about the bustling street nestled among the pine trees and blue peaks of the Rocky Mountains and nodded her approval.

"Anywhere you say," she agreed.

He grinned at her. "You look so different."

"I am different. Wait until I tell you about my clothing. I hope you're not shocked."

He grinned. "Not a thing you can say or do will shock me. I'm the one who knows you, remember?"

"Yes, and I'm the one who recognized you were a good man before even you did."

"I still got some bad."

She lifted her eyebrows in speculation and gave him a lustful look that burned him up like a spent matchstick.

"I hope so. I'm looking forward to riding double with you very soon."

His ears went hot as the memories of their night ride poured through him, bringing him to an arousal very inappropriate for a public street.

"First I aim to marry you."

She smiled, her eyes twinkling with delight. "I thought you'd never ask. Yes, Mr. Boon, I'd be honored to be your wife."

He gathered her up and kissed her hard. Gunfire sounded and hollering. Someone shouted, "The sheriff's found himself a girl!"

He pulled back to see the gathering of curious citizens. He pointed at the ones with raised weapons and motioned to his own holster. The firearms disappeared.

"Wife," he corrected. "The sheriff found himself a wife."

Chapter Twenty-Three

Laurie had taken to calling her fiancé Justice. It suited him perfectly. And, as they were to be married, he needed a last name to offer his bride. Justice surprised Laurie by wanting to marry properly in a church with friends and family. Laurie had invited her parents and Boon invited the friends he'd made in Silver Cliff. He had also insisted she wear white, saying that she was pure as snow and he wouldn't hear any different. She'd finished her gown just before her parents arrived at the station.

The wedding had been perfect, the supper overly long. But finally she was alone with her husband and all that separated them was a trifold screen and the length of the bedroom in the small house that came as part and parcel with his position in Silver Cliff.

Laurie Garcia Bender Boon removed her petticoats, bloomers, stockings, corset and shift all from behind the screen. The splashing she heard on the other side told her that he made use of the washbasin. The scraping that followed caused her to cock her head.

"Are you shaving?" she asked.

"Yes."

"At night?"

"Don't want my whiskers to mark your fine skin."

The idea of his scratchy cheek grazing over her inner thigh caused her breath to catch. She hurriedly burrowed into the sheer lace gown that combined femininity and daring. Laurie paused to stare at herself in the oval mirror.

Pins still captured her hair in an elegant upsweep. Her cheeks were flushed in anticipation and she could see the dark outline of her nipples through the lace.

"Justice?" She liked the sound of his new given name as much as she liked being Mrs. Justice Boon. Tonight she would go to him without regret because she was his wife.

"Hmmm?" he answered.

"I'm ready."

Something clattered against porcelain. A moment later came the sound of running feet as her husband charged across the room. Next came the squeak of the ropes beneath the mattress.

She giggled, picturing him diving headfirst into their marriage bed.

She wondered what he'd do if she dove right in after him, for she was equally eager for their wedding night to begin. Through his love and his unconditional acceptance she now truly believed she had nothing of which to be ashamed. Her past experience was a mistake or perhaps a crime, as her husband insisted. He was adamant that she was no more at fault than the victim of a robbery. He said he didn't miss what she lacked and any man who did was "a damned fool." Besides, he said he wouldn't know what to do with a scared virgin on her wedding night. That last comment was one of the sweetest things he'd ever said, because she was certain he spoke to alleviate her sorrow at not being able to come to him as pure as her white dress. But she believed he really didn't care.

Laurie stroked the train of her wedding gown, now hanging over the screen. This was the first dress she had made since turning her attention to riding skirts and she was proud of her efforts. She'd never forget the look on Justice's face when he first saw her in this dress, all wonder and gratitude. She felt just the same to find her tall, handsome husband-to-be waiting for her beside the altar.

Justice had helped her with the long row of pearl buttons that descended down her spine, punctuating each one with a tiny kiss at her shoulder and neck until she was tingling and aroused and aching to have him. He'd been reluctant to release her. His demanding kiss and command that she "hurry back" had changed her mind about the need for nightclothes. But he'd given her a push toward the screen, saying that he wanted to see what she had been sewing out of all that lace, as her gown contained none of it. Strictly ivory satin and silk roses with a bustle and train that made walking nearly impossible, but did lengthen the waistline dramatically in the modern style.

She stared down at the circle of gold on her left ring finger. The gold filigree band was set with three diamonds. The perfect symbol of the bright future they would share. Laurie extinguished the lamp on the dressing stand.

"Laurie?" He sounded fretful, impatient. Eager.

She smiled as anticipation curled inside her and stepped from behind the screen. Boon had the lamp beside the bed turned down so the golden light gilded the taut skin of his bare chest. The sight stole her breath away. Her gaze wandered to where the covers pooled at his waist and her brow lifted in speculation at the interesting tenting of the bedding.

Their eyes met. His sharp intake of air made her smile.

"I'm the luckiest bastard in the world," he said.

She knitted her brow. "Don't call yourself that. You're a lawman, a respected member of this community and my husband."

His shy smile held a hint of pride. "Still getting used to all that."

Laurie made him wait, lifting her arms and removing her hairpins one by one while her husband devoured her with his eyes.

"It's like you're wrapped in a bridal veil."

"It's the same fabric," she said.

"If I die right now I won't have far to go. I'm already in heaven."

She shook out her hair, letting it tumble all about her bare shoulders. Justice flipped back the covers, recalled he was naked and flicked them back. His gaze flashed to hers, his intent stare searching for her reaction.

Her lips curled in a sensual smile. “Not a scared virgin. Remember?”

“Come here, wife,” he ordered.

She did, gladly, padding silently across the floor, closing the distance between them. The rightness of this struck her hard as he enfolded her in his arms. She lay beside him on their marriage bed inhaling the heady aroma of soap, leather and the scent that was uniquely his own. Laurie clung, pressing against his side as his hand swept down her back.

“I want to keep the lamp burning. I want to see you when we share this bed.”

She nodded her acceptance as her fingers grazed over the soft skin, exploring the chiseled muscle of his chest. Amazed, she noted his nipple hardening at her touch. A tingle of anticipation rippled along her spine. What other surprises awaited her?

Laurie lifted her gaze to meet his, finding him biting his lower lip. She tilted her chin and he swept in to kiss her long and hard. His tongue grazed her lips and then danced with hers as he took her to the bed. His biceps bulged as he drew back, resting on his elbows.

"Laurie, do you want babies right away or would you like a little time?"

She didn't hesitate, knowing exactly what she wanted. "Right away. I want everything right away."

He grinned. "All right then."

Boon stroked her neck and drew away the lace that shielded her breasts from his lips. His kisses descended and Laurie's body responded. She ached for him deep down within herself. Laurie lifted her hips and finished removing her frilly nightdress, thinking that from this day on she'd come to their bed naked.

Boon used the gathered lace to stroke her needy body, brushing her skin until she arched and clung. She tried to draw him on top of her, spreading her legs in welcome, but he slipped away, using his smooth cheek and clever tongue on her abdomen and then her inner thigh.

Laurie forgot how to breathe as his fingers delved into the thick nest of dark hair between her legs. She remembered that first night when they rode double on a fast horse and Boon had touched her here. Anticipation curled, only this time she felt not one moment's embarrassment. The awkwardness had been replaced with eagerness; the shame with anticipation. He loved her and she loved him so nothing they did together could ever be wrong. She knew that now, deep in her heart, and felt the rightness of this joining. She lifted her hips to meet his delving fingers, his expert tongue.

She clutched the bedding, his hair, the bedposts, as she tossed her head and lifted to meet each exquisite stroke. Her passion built. Gasps and moans and sounds that were not quite words all tore from her. He only increased his pace and she knew he had the endurance that had carried her to safety and would now carry her home.

This time she did not try to staunch the rising tide of pleasure. Instead she threw herself into the void, trusting her husband to support her weight as the rippling contractions burst through her. She arched meeting the pleasure and then collapsed with the retreating waves. Boon lifted his dark head, slid his slippery mouth over her inner thigh and then scaled her body until his erection pressed hard against her soft belly. He wrapped her in his arms and kissed her, his mouth now tasting salty, and she realized that she tasted him and herself together on his lips.

A thrill of excitement beat inside her at what they would do next. She wanted to give Boon everything she could and knew that he offered the same. But her legs trembled and her limbs had gone limp as an old rag doll's.

His kisses were soft at first, but relentless, as her husband continued to lick and kiss. When he reached her earlobe, she groaned half in reluctance, accepting the building craving he rekindled.

Curiosity tantalized her. She was wet and wanting. Laurie reached down and captured the object of her desire in her hand.

Boon stiffened and drew a long breath. She loosened her grip and slid her palm up and down the lovely, long length of him. His skin was soft as velvet, but oh, my, the difference between that texture and what lay beneath.

He extended his arms and stared down at her. She glanced at the prize she had captured and then met his eyes.

"Come here, husband," she commanded.

One side of Boon's mouth twitched upward. "Yes, ma'am."

He settled between her open thighs and she placed both feet on the mattress, angling her hips to meet him. He paused there a moment, just outside her body. She gripped his taut backside and pulled. Boon's eyes never left hers as he slipped inside and slid home inch by satisfying inch. Their hips locked. He waited. She wrapped her legs behind his lower back and squeezed. He withdrew and began a slow steady rhythm meant solely to drive her to distraction. Laurie's eyes widened as she felt the now familiar building of desire. Boon smiled and increased his pace. Like a mustang, her husband had good wind and an excellent, smooth gait. The pleasure overtook her again and she arched against the mattress, giving a long moan as her release danced outward from where their bodies met.

When she opened her eyes, it was to see the fracturing of her husband's unbreakable control. Like a wild horse feeling the cinch or a cow scorched by the branding iron, he broke into a wild, riotous bucking that lengthened Laurie's pleasure and had her gasping for breath. He arched his back and gasped. She stared up in wonder at the expression of rapture so intent it bordered on anguish. She stilled and stared and then felt the surge of his release.

Laurie could not draw air fast enough. She used the last of her dwindling reserve to encircle her arms about his neck as he rolled to his back, carrying her along to sprawl across his wide chest. She held him as his ragged breath blew soft against her neck and the dampness of their skin cooled in the still dry air.

"That was the most breathtaking, soul-shattering experience of my life," she whispered.

Boon lifted up to one elbow. His hair now fell down over his forehead. She swept it back and then caressed his smooth cheek.

"I love you, Laurie. I'm so proud to have you as my wife."

She crumbled inside, knowing it was true and feeling so very grateful.

At her change of expression, a line formed between his dark brows. "Laurie?"

"I wanted to marry a respectable man but I never believed I deserved one as fine as you."

He started to speak but she pressed two fingers to his lips.

"Justice, you saved me twice. First from those outlaws and now you've given me a life that I only ever touched in my dreams. I didn't believe I deserved this or could ever have a husband as decent as you are. But you changed all that. You told me I was worthy and I believed you. I want to make you so proud of me because I am *so* proud of you." The tears blurred her vision and he kissed them away.

Boon rolled to his back and gathered her up

so she lay pressed to his side, her head upon his wide capable shoulders.

"I already am," he said. "And not just because you're beautiful. I love you through and through, both the iron and the lace. Never knew a female could be hard and soft all at once. Most are one or t'other. But you're all that and now you're mine."

She raised her chin to look up at her husband. Her heart spilled over with joy. The certainty in his eyes and the hope in her heart held them fast, would hold them fast for the many years to come. For this was only the night of the first day of the long and respectable marriage of the respectable Mister and Mrs. Justice Boon.

* * * * *